ELEPHANT THUN...

Elizabeth Laird was born in New Zealand but when she was three the family moved to England. Since then she has travelled to the furthest corners of the world and has encountered all kinds of animals. On one adventure she became lost at night in a Kenyan game reserve, coming a little too close to an angry rhino and narrowly avoiding buffalo and elephants. Her experience of the wild animals of Africa has helped her write the *Wild Things* series.

She is the award-winning author of *Red Sky in the Morning*, *Kiss the Dust*, *Secret Friends* (shortlisted for the 1997 Carnegie Medal) and many other children's novels.

Elizabeth Laird has been helped in her research for *Wild Things* by wildlife experts and local people in Kenya, whose lives are constantly touched by the animals amongst which they live.

Books available in the Wild Things series

1. Leopard Trail
2. Baboon Rock
3. Elephant Thunder

Coming soon

4. Rhino Fire   August 1999
5. Red Wolf   October 1999

All Wild Things titles can be ordered at your local bookshop or are available by post from Book Service by Post (tel: 01624 675137).

WILD THINGS

ELEPHANT THUNDER

Elizabeth Laird

MACMILLAN CHILDREN'S BOOKS

Series consultant: Dr Shirley Strum
with the support of Dr David Western,
past director of the Kenya Wildlife Service

JF

First published 1999 by Macmillan Children's Books
a division of Macmillan Publishers Limited
25 Eccleston Place, London SW1W 9NF
Basingstoke and Oxford

Associated companies throughout the world

ISBN 0 330 37150 9

1 3 5 7 9 8 6 4 2

A CIP catalogue record for this book is available from
the British Library.

Phototypeset by Intype London Ltd
Printed and bound in Great Britain by Mackays of Chatham plc, Kent

Silence hung over the forest clearing. In the heavy heat of midday, a leopard rested in the high branches of a giant fig tree, and even the birds were still.

Soft footfalls sounded up the track. A wary monkey turned her head. Fourteen elephants were converging on the clearing, six from one side and eight from the other, rocking from side to side with each deliberate step, and calling to each other as they came, with deep rumbling signals.

The monkey relaxed. She had nothing to fear from them.

The elephants came out into the clearing and began to greet one another, the older females lifting their trunks to touch their friends' faces, the younger ones coiling their trunks together in loving knots.

Two young bulls caught sight of each other and with shrill trumpetings began to wrestle, their heads raised, their trunks rolled back like whips, ready to strike. They began to tussle with their tusks, and the clash of ivory rang out through the forest. Then they laid their trunks against each

1

other's foreheads and began to push, staggering backwards and forwards in a giant trial of strength.

Neither of them saw the baby elephant nearby. She had wandered towards them away from her mother, attracted by the fight. The bigger of the two young males, lurching backwards, kicked the baby accidentally with his great rear foot. The baby's shrill scream brought her mother, a huge matriarch, lunging across the clearing, trumpeting furiously.

Both males turned, and as they did so, one caught the other's head with the sharp point of his tusk, gouging a deep wound in the sensitive skin near his eye.

The wounded elephant roared, shook his head, and began trampling violently about. The baby's mother pushed him impatiently aside, reached out for her calf with her trunk, laid it tenderly against her and nudged her out of harm's way. Then she stood, tall and angry, confronting the two young males, flapping her great ears and waving her head threateningly to and fro.

For some time now, the young elephant bulls had been growing too strong and excitable, too prone to jostle the females and fight each other. It was time for them to leave the herd of cows and calves, to break away from their mothers and aunts and small brothers and sisters. They would have to learn to go off and fend for themselves, to fight for their place among the hierarchy of bulls.

The unhurt elephant wheeled away and trotted out of the clearing, but the wounded one, defiant and sore, stood his ground. The females angrily bunched together, drawing their little ones under the great shelters of their bodies.

The young wounded male waved his trunk and flapped his ears. He was hurt and he wanted to be comforted. But no comfort was forthcoming for him now. Angry and in pain, he gave a defiant roar, but the females were unmoved. Furiously, the young bull wheeled round and charged a little way away, trumpeting out his rage as he crashed noisily through the undergrowth, then he turned and stood uncertainly, watching the females, waiting for a sign from them. Ignoring him, they began to walk quietly away, and he was left alone.

1

AN UNWELCOME GUEST

'Who is Kelly-Ann, anyway?' said Tom, staring resentfully at his mother.

Debbie Wilkinson got awkwardly to her feet. Her baby was due in a few weeks' time and she was feeling clumsy and irritable.

'You know perfectly well who Kelly-Ann is,' she snapped. 'She came round with her mum last week. Julie, remember? Dad's assistant at Murchisons.'

'I didn't see them. I wasn't here.'

'No, come to think of it, you weren't, were you?' Debbie sounded sarcastic. 'You'd slipped off next door, hadn't you? To those two precious friends of yours!'

Tom didn't answer.

'I thought Kelly-Ann was a very nice little girl,' Debbie went on. 'She's not much younger than you, after all.'

'Mum! She's ten!'

'Nearly eleven. And you're only twelve.'

Tom slumped back into his chair and kicked the coffee table with his foot.

'Why'd you go and invite her for the weekend? I mean, the weekend!'

'I didn't invite her. Julie asked if we could have her. She's got a new boyfriend and they want to go down to the coast. I couldn't exactly say no, could I?'

'Don't see why not.'

'She won't be any trouble. She'll be someone for you to play with.'

'I've got friends of my own, thank you very much,' said Tom stiffly.

He'd been balancing his football on his knees. Now he started punching it from one hand to the other.

'Anyway, why did you have to give her my room?'

'Oh Tom, we've been through all this before.' Debbie was standing at the table at the far end of the sitting room unpacking a bag. 'It's not your room now. It's the baby's. We moved your stuff out last week. Kelly-Ann'll only be here for two nights and she'll need to be near me and Dad in the night. It'll be her first time away from her mum, and anyway, they've only been in Africa for a couple of months. She's bound to be a bit scared.'

'I'm not scared. I'm not scared,' said a high-pitched voice behind Tom. He groaned inwardly. He'd thought that Bella, his three-year-old sister and the bane of his life, was still having her afternoon rest.

'No, sweetheart, of course you're not scared,' said Debbie.

'No sweetheart, of course you're not scared,' mimicked Tom, half under his breath.

He threw the football a little harder than he'd intended, and failed to catch it. It bounced across the floor and hit Bella on the leg. She opened her mouth, ready to scream, then noticed what her mother was unpacking.

'Little rabbits!' she said. 'Can I have those rabbits?'

The yellow rabbits were printed on material that Debbie was holding up admiringly.

'No, darling. Look, they're the curtains for the baby's room,' she said. 'Baby will like them, won't she, Bella?'

Behind their backs, Tom pretended to be sick. Then he realized what Debbie had said.

'She?' he demanded. '*She*? How do you know it's a girl? If it is, that's it. I'm going. I'm leaving home.'

'Oh don't be silly, Tom,' said Debbie. She turned and nearly fell over the football. 'And for heaven's sake get that ball out of here. I've told you a hundred times, I'm up to here with it. Next time I'll—'

She gave a little scream. A tiny bird had swooped in through the open verandah doors, its outstretched wings scything the air, its black forked tail turning as deftly as a rudder.

Bella yelled with fright. Debbie started back. Tom held out his hand invitingly.

'Jonathan!' he breathed. 'Jonathan Swift! You're back!'

The swift landed on Tom's hand and sidled up to his shoulder.

Debbie stared in amazement.

'What is this?' she demanded. 'What's going on? Is it one of Afra's tricks? Living next door to that child is as bad as being in a menagerie.'

'Afra's house isn't a menagerie,' said Tom, speaking in a fierce whisper so as not to startle the swift. 'It's a . . . a haven for orphans. Jonathan's an orphan. As good as, anyway. He fell out of his nest and Afra's bringing him up. Brought him up. He flew away and now he's back.'

He laughed as the swift hopped right up to his face and nuzzled his nose with his beak. 'Hey, Jon boy, that tickles!'

Bella had been clinging tightly to Debbie's hand. She suddenly let go of it and ran up Tom.

'I want to hold him,' she said. 'Give him to me.'

Startled, the swift flew off Tom's shoulder and landed on the table. Debbie flapped her hands at him. The swift lifted his tail and a stream of white goo shot out over the rabbit curtain material.

Debbie started back and exclaimed with

disgust. Tom sniggered. His mother turned on him furiously.

'Out,' she said. 'I've had enough. You can do what I told you this morning, Tom. Get that mess of yours out of the cupboard in the baby's room and sort out your new room. Dad's bringing Kelly-Ann back with him from work. They'll be here soon.'

The swift took fright at her loud voice and in a flurry of wings dived out through the verandah doors. Tom's good temper went with the bird and he started feeling angry again.

'What mess?' he said. 'That's not mess. That's my stuff. And there isn't anywhere to put it in the other room. It's a horrible room anyway, and there's no cupboards in it or anything, and it's all dark and depressing and you can't see out of the window because of that huge tree. I can't even see into Afra's garden.'

'Just as well.' Debbie was scrubbing crossly at the mess on the new curtains. 'I've had enough of that young lady and her precious friend. Every time you get together with Afra and Joseph there's some silly business with some animal or other, bringing dirt and germs into the house. Just look at this! The material's ruined!'

'Good,' mouthed Tom. He couldn't bear it. Unfortunately, Debbie had looked up at the wrong moment and had read his lips.

'If I have to tell you one more time . . .' she began, an angry flush mounting her cheeks.

'OK, don't rupture yourself,' said Tom rudely.

He picked up his football, marched to the door and, resisting the urge to boot Bella out of his way, went out of the room letting the door bang loudly after him.

'Tom!' he heard his mother shout angrily, but he took no notice, opened the front door and ran out of the house.

A few moments later, he was in the garden next door. Afra Tovey was sitting on the steps of the verandah at the back of the house with a bush-baby curled up in her lap, fast asleep.

'Tom!' she said, looking up. 'What are you doing here? I thought you had company coming today?'

'Company!' said Tom bitterly. 'I wouldn't call her company. Sweet little diddums Kelly-Ann. I'll probably strangle her after a while and then I'll have to go to prison for the rest of my life.'

Afra grinned at him.

'Maybe she won't be that bad,' she said.

The bushbaby stirred and opened one huge eye.

'That's good,' said Afra, lovingly stroking the soft hair on his underbelly. 'You'll feel better soon, Kiksy.'

Tom looked down at the furry little creature.

'Why? What's the matter with him?'

'I wish I knew.' Afra looked anxious.

'He looks all right to me.'

From somewhere in the bungalow behind, Tom heard a door opening and shutting.

'Where's Joseph?' he said. 'Thought we could have a game of football or something.'

He bounced the ball, caught it on his foot and kicked it back up into his hand. The bushbaby moved listlessly in Afra's lap.

'Hey, watch out,' said Afra sharply. 'You'll alarm Kiksy.'

She picked up a piece of banana from the plate beside her and offered it to the little creature. He turned his head away.

'Maybe he's just tired,' said Tom. 'Isn't he supposed to sleep all day and be awake all night?'

'Yes, but he's sick.' Afra gently tapped the bushbaby's head. 'Look at him.'

Tom looked. Kiksy lay limply in Afra's hands, his eyes closed, his breath coming fast.

'What are you going to do?'

'I guess I'll wait a bit. He was bad like this once before but he just kind of bounced back. Maybe he ate something.'

She lifted the bushbaby's head and offered him the banana again.

'Come on, baby. Eat.'

The word baby flicked Tom on the raw. He looked away.

'Where's Joseph?' he said again.

Afra jerked her head towards the house.

'In the kitchen. His Uncle Titus is here.'

'What?' Tom brightened at once. 'Why didn't you say so before?'

He hurried round the side of the house to the kitchen door. Joseph Musau, the son of the Toveys' housekeeper, was sitting at the table talking in rapid Swahili to his uncle, a tall African, whose long strong hands sliced the air as he spoke.

'Hello!' said Tom, bounding in through the door. Titus Musau worked for the Kenya Wildlife Service. He had been chased by rhinos, hunted by lions and had once even been bitten by a snake. Tom thought he was great.

Titus turned in his chair and stretched out his arm to punch Tom lightly on the shoulder.

'Tom! How are you? Joseph was talking about you just now.'

'What was he saying?' Tom looked a little anxious. Joseph burst out laughing.

'Eh, heh, Tom, you should see your own face. I'm telling Uncle Titus you have a criminal mentality, a serious personality disorder, a . . .'

Titus silenced his nephew with a wave of his hand.

'You're an animal man, is that right, Tom? A big game fan – and I don't mean football games. Listen, I have to go to Meru tomorrow. There's a problem with elephants there. How long have you been in Africa now? Eight months? Nine months?

And you've never seen elephants? This fellow' – he clapped Joseph on the shoulder – 'is coming to Meru with me. I'm going to take him out on my elephant monitoring drive. How would you like to come too?'

Tom's face lit up.

'Elephants?' He said. '*Elephants?* I'd love to come.' He stopped and his face darkened again. 'I can't,' he went on bitterly. 'My mum's invited this kid to stay for the weekend and I'm supposed to be looking after her.'

Titus nodded.

'Then you must stay,' he said matter-of-factly. 'I'm sorry. Now, Joseph, has Afra made her mind up? Is she coming with us?'

Joseph shook his head.

'No,' he said. 'She's too worried about Kiksy. He's sick. She might have to take him to the vet.'

'I see.' Titus picked up his jacket. 'Joseph, I'll come and collect you tomorrow morning, early. Oh, and take something warm. It's cold up there around Mount Kenya.'

He went out of the room. Tom banged his fist down on the table. The pile of vegetables that Sarah had left on it bounced and rolled, threatening to fall onto the floor.

'It's so unfair,' Tom burst out. 'First I have to give my room up, then there's this creepy girl I've got to go around with for the whole weekend, and now I can't even come to Meru with you.'

Joseph frowned, trying to disentangle all this. He latched on to the first bit.

'You've moved out of your room? Why?'

'Mum says she needs it for the new baby.'

Joseph looked out of the window and said nothing. Tom suddenly felt uncomfortable. Joseph shared a tiny house with his mother, Sarah. It consisted only of two cramped little rooms behind the Toveys' old ramshackle bungalow. Joseph had never had a room of his own in his whole life. Guilt made Tom angrier than ever.

'Well, are you going to play football or aren't you?' he demanded.

Joseph reached out and in one lightning move prised the football out of Tom's hands and ran out of the kitchen.

There was a patch of overgrown grass behind the bungalow. Tom raced after Joseph, roughly tackled him and got possession of the ball. He pulled back his leg, then packing into his foot all the fury and frustration of the afternoon, kicked it as hard as he could. The ball sailed up and up, grazing the outer branches of a mango tree that stood between the Toveys' and Wilkinsons' gardens, and startling a flock of starlings that twittered and fluttered in fright, flashing their iridescent blue wings. Then, as the boys watched in silent horror, it flew towards the round window of Tom's old bedroom, as straight as a well-aimed cannon ball, and crashed right through it, with a loud explosion of breaking glass.

Tom and Joseph looked at each other.

'That was the best kick you have ever kicked,' said Joseph, awestruck.

'She'll kill me. She really, really will,' said Tom.

He could hear Bella already, screaming at the top of her voice, and Debbie shouting furiously.

'I'd better go,' he said to Joseph, and began walking slowly up the Toveys' garden towards the front gate.

He turned in through his own front gate. Debbie was already marching up the path towards him, her face red with fury.

'How dare you? How dare you!' she shouted at him. 'Just wait till your father hears about this.'

'I didn't mean—' began Tom.

A new kind of scream, louder than any that Bella had made before, came from inside the house and made them both turn their heads.

'You wait,' Debbie hissed at Tom. 'You just wait.'

She turned and ran heavily back into the house. Tom followed slowly. He reached the open front door in time to see his mother coming down the stairs again with Bella in her arms. Blood was flowing from a gash in Bella's leg.

'Look what you've done!' Debbie shouted at him. 'She's cut herself on all that broken glass.'

'What was she doing in my room, then?' Tom

yelled back, feeling the blood pumping up into his head. 'I've told her again and again, she's not allowed in there.'

'It's *not* your room. It's the baby's! You don't deserve a room at all. You deserve a damn good hiding!' Debbie was almost hysterical. 'Now get upstairs and clear up the mess. Do you hear me? Get out of my sight!'

She stopped. She was looking out over Tom's head. A car was turning in through the gate.

'Oh no, I can't bear it. Here's your father and Kelly-Ann already. Tom? Tom!'

But Tom had fled past her up the stairs and locked himself into his old room.

2

AN ANGRY QUARREL

With the door of his old room shut, Tom couldn't hear much of what was going on downstairs. He picked up as much broken glass as he could see. It was everywhere. Splinters of it were embedded in the rug and the wooden floor, and were lying on the bed which Debbie had made up for Kelly-Ann. Without a dustpan and brush it was impossible to do the job thoroughly.

After a long time, he heard heavy footsteps coming up the stairs.

Dad! he thought, breaking out into a sweat.

The door handle turned.

'Tom!' The tone of Simon Wilkinson's voice was hard to interpret. 'Open this door at once.'

For about two seconds, Tom considered the possibility of keeping his door locked for ever and staying in the room until he starved to death, but he thought better of it, went over to the door and unlocked it.

To his surprise, his father looked quite calm.

'A football, was it?' he said, his voice almost sympathetic. 'Where did you kick from?'

'Afra's garden,' mumbled Tom.

Simon looked out through the empty window frame and whistled.

'Must have been a quite a kick.' He cleared his throat and tried to look stern. 'Have you cleared it up properly?'

'I don't know. I need the broom and stuff.'

'I brought it up,' said his father. 'Go along to your new room and keep your head down for a bit. I'll finish up here.'

'What about the window?'

'We'll stick something over it for tonight. I'll get someone round to fix it tomorrow. Now push off.'

Tom walked down the landing to his poky new room and opened the door. The tree that overhung his window made the room dark, but he could hardly fail to see that a skinny little girl in a pink dress and white cotton socks was sitting on his bed. She looked up at him.

'Hello,' she said.

He was taken by surprise.

'What are you doing in here?'

'Debbie says not to go into my bedroom until the glass is all cleared up.'

She was leafing through his book of football stickers.

She must've opened the drawer in my desk to find that, thought Tom with a shock of indignation.

He marched over to her and took the book out of her hands.

'Excuse me,' he said. 'That's private.'

'Why?' said Kelly-Ann. 'They're only boring old football stickers.'

She was looking round the room, appraising Tom's things. He wanted to pick her up and throw her bodily out through the door.

'Oo!' she squealed suddenly, pushing her straight blond hair out of her eyes and pointing up at the elephant poster that Titus had given him. 'Elephants! I love elephants. They're so cute.'

'You think elephants are cute?'

Tom glanced up at the magnificent poster of a bull elephant that he had stuck above his bed. Its great ears were extended and its huge tusks raised to the sky. It stood proudly against the golden vastness of Africa, dwarfing everything around it. He looked down disgustedly at Kelly-Ann. She stared back at him, her sharp little eyes assessing him. Then she smiled, looking pleased with herself.

'Yeah. I've got a piggy bank elephant at home. It's got all blue flowers on it.'

'Has it really?' Tom tried to keep the sarcasm out of his voice. He had to coexist with this awful person for an entire weekend. He'd try not to murder her just yet.

He looked across at the window and had an

idea. He went over to it, opened it and leaned out.

'What are you doing?' said Kelly-Ann.

'Just checking.' Tom turned away from the window, leaving it open. 'There are big green snakes in this tree sometimes. They lie in wait for birds. Sometimes they wriggle out onto the roof and try to get in through the other upstairs windows.'

Kelly-Ann was gaping at him, her mouth a round O of horror.

'It's not true. I'll ask Debbie.'

'Don't do that,' said Tom hastily. 'She hates snakes. If she gets a fright she'll have the baby early or something. Then you'd be in trouble.'

Kelly-Ann shut her mouth again and sidled to the door.

'I'm going to find Bella,' she said. 'She's cute. I brought her a present. A toy rabbit.'

'Good,' said Tom, ushering her firmly to the door. 'I know for a fact that she's crazy about rabbits.'

He shut the door after her and slumped down onto his bed. A cool breeze came in through the window, rustling the heavy dark leaves of the tree outside. He turned his head and stared idly at them, then suddenly sat bolt upright. A small green eye was gazing unwinkingly at him.

For a moment he stared at it, unable to make

out what it was, his heart beating a little faster. What if there really were snakes in the tree? Then a pair of lids closed slowly over the eye, one coming down from above, the other coming up to meet it from below, and he relaxed again. It was only a chameleon after all, its colour so perfectly matching the leaves and branches around it that it was pure fluke that he'd seen it at all.

He stood up to get a closer look. The chameleon's back was nubbly with lumps and bumps, and its tail was curled around a twig like a spring. Its feet were like real hands, with toes just like fingers, that were splayed out as if it was about to play the piano.

Tom leaned over to check if its tummy was the same colour as its back, but his sudden movement startled the chameleon and it scuttled away into the deep foliage of the tree. Tom looked carefully but he couldn't see it now. He felt a bit better. Having chameleons outside the window was one thing to be said about this awful room. He was still furious with everyone, though.

The room was over the kitchen and from downstairs he could hear the clatter of crockery. They must be getting the supper ready. He didn't care. He wasn't hungry.

He lay down on his bed again and looked at the elephant poster. It seemed to draw him in. He could almost catch a whiff of the giant animal's sweet warm smell and hear the measured swish of its feet through the yellow grass. The great creature looked so strong and proud, so lonely and noble, that it made Tom feel sad. He'd seen a film once about poachers slaughtering elephants for their tusks. This elephant looked as if it was the last survivor of a massacre, a solitary ranger over the vastness of Africa.

'At least you've got a bit of privacy, mate,' said Tom out loud. 'At least you haven't got this lot on your back.'

'Tom! Tom!' His mother was calling him. 'Come down here. Supper's ready.'

His heart sank. She'd be bound to go on at him about everything in general and broken windows in particular. He sighed, got up and went downstairs.

Kelly-Ann was already sitting on a chair at the kitchen table with Bella on her knee, reading her a story. Bella was gazing up at Kelly-Ann adoringly.

'Sit down,' said Debbie tersely, frowning at Tom.

He sat down. His dad came into the room.

'Well, this is nice,' he said breezily, looking round the table. 'What's for supper?'

'Chicken casserole,' said Debbie, lifting a pot from the cooker to the table.

Kelly-Ann looked up.

'Didn't Mum tell you, Debbie? I'm vegetarian.'

There was a short silence.

'No,' said Debbie. 'No, she didn't tell me. Well,

love, you'll just have to eat the potatoes and veg and I'll do you a fried egg.'

'I don't like eggs,' said Kelly-Ann.

Simon took the lid off the casserole and put out his hand for Tom's plate. Tom stopped himself grinning and decided that he was hungry after all.

Debbie rolled her eyes towards Simon. He was too busy ladling out the casserole to notice. She rounded on Tom.

'Get the cheese out for Kelly-Ann,' she said.

Tom looked hopefully at Kelly-Ann. Perhaps she didn't like cheese, either. But Kelly-Ann was smiling up at Debbie, her big blue eyes sickly with gratitude.

'Oh thank you, Debbie. Mum said I wasn't to be a nuisance with my fads and fancies, but I'm not a nuisance, am I?'

'Course not, dear!' said Debbie, a little too heartily, sitting down herself. 'Now, Bella, get off Kelly-Ann's lap. Get on to your own chair and eat your supper.'

'I don't like chicken,' said Bella experiment-ally. 'I only like biscuits.'

'That's enough.' Debbie's voice was sharp. 'Be quiet and eat up.'

As soon as supper was over, Tom slipped out of the kitchen through the back door into the garden. He wanted to get out, to be next door with his friends. He'd had enough of his family.

A little black cat trotted out of the velvety darkness and began to coil herself round his feet.

'Tiger,' said Tom, and he bent down to tickle her under her chin in the spot she loved best.

The door behind him opened.

'Tom? Where do you think you're going?'

It was his mother. Tom said nothing. Debbie stepped out of the house and shut the door behind her.

'You're staying right here,' she said. 'I want a word with you.'

Tom picked Tiger up, holding her a little too tightly. She miaowed in protest.

'Look, love.' Debbie put a hand into the small of her back as if to ease an ache. She lowered her voice, making an effort, in spite of her tiredness, to sound conciliatory. 'I know it's been hard for you, giving up your room and having Kelly-Ann here for the weekend, but there's no need to make it difficult for everyone else. You can't have it your own way all the time. There are other members of the family to be considered, you know.'

Tiger struggled free, leapt out of Tom's arms and ran off into the darkness. Tom looked down at the ground. He could feel his temper rising inside him like a red wave.

'You're old enough now to start taking a bit of responsibility,' Debbie went on. 'Giving me a hand with the shopping. Not disappearing next door all the time. Helping me with Bella occasion-ally—'

'I don't go next door all the time,' Tom broke in, trying to keep the anger out of his voice. 'And Bella never does what I tell her.'

'Keeping your room tidy,' Debbie went on inexorably. 'Just because we've got help in the house here, it doesn't mean you can treat it like a pigsty.' Her indignation was growing and her voice was rising.

The red wave rose up into Tom's head, and broke in a surge of anger.

'That so unfair!' he burst out. 'You're always going on at me. You never let me do what I want. You let Bella get away with murder. Everything's always my fault. Now I'm supposed to put up with this stupid girl. You never asked what I felt about it. You don't give a stuff about me at all.'

'Don't you speak to me like that!' Debbie was losing her temper too. 'I've just about had enough of this, Tom. You're selfish and lazy, irresponsible and—'

'And you're a fat cow and I hate you!' shouted Tom, the wave of anger swamping him altogether.

Debbie gasped and put her hand up to her mouth. She stepped back as if Tom had hit her.

'How – how could you?' she said in a low voice.

Tom was trembling all over. He shot a quick

glance at Debbie's face but she wasn't looking at him.

'Tiger's gone off somewhere,' she said, her voice thickened with tears. 'I'll go and look for her.'

Then she walked away into the dark garden.

The red wave had subsided now and Tom looked after her miserably. He hadn't meant to say that. He felt bad, as if he'd let himself down.

Why does everything always go wrong? he thought. He heard something behind him and turned round. Afra and Joseph had been standing in the shadows. They stepped forward into the light that streamed out of the kitchen window and Tom could see by their faces that they'd heard what he'd said.

'We came to say hi to Kelly-Ann,' said Afra in a tight voice. She glanced quickly up at him, then looked down again. Beside her, Joseph stood as silent and rigid as a pole, his face impossible to read in the darkness.

'Kelly-Ann? What d'you want to see her for?' said Tom, wishing for once that his friends weren't there. He nodded towards the kitchen door. 'She's in there.'

Afra pushed past him and opened the door. Bella, who worshipped Afra with a devotion that never failed to irritate Tom, ran up to her and flung her arms round Afra's knees. Afra picked her up and looked across to Kelly-Ann.

'Hi,' she said. 'I'm Afra, from next door. This is Joseph.'

At that moment, a piercing scream came from outside. Tiger shot in through the door, a wild black streak of terror, and Debbie stumbled into the kitchen after him. Simon, who had been sitting at the table with the newspaper in front of him, ran across to her.

'What is it? What happened?'

'A snake!' panted Debbie, her voice shaking with fright. 'A big one. Near the mango tree. I nearly stepped on it. Oh Simon, I got such a fright. Oh, I feel – I feel terrible.'

'I'll get you a glass of water,' said Simon, wrenching open the cupboard to get at the glasses.

'No, I . . .' said Debbie weakly. Then she collapsed onto a chair and fainted.

'Debs! Debs!' Simon stood helplessly, a glass in his hand, staring in horror at the deathly pale face of his wife. Bella started to cry noisily and struggled out of Afra's arms. Tom felt as if he was living through a nightmare.

'Call the doctor, Dad,' he heard himself say.

'Yes, of course! Put her feet up. Get her head down.'

He ran out of the room.

Joseph shot a fierce look at Tom, then turned to Afra.

'I'll go and get Ma,' he said.

They opened the door, but stepped back as

Titus, followed by his sister, Sarah, came into the kitchen.

'We heard some screaming,' said Sarah, her broad brown face wrinkled with concern. 'Is somebody hurt?'

'It was a snake in the garden,' Afra said. 'Tom's mum saw it. She's fainted.'

Sarah went over to Debbie and crouched down beside her, patting her hands gently. Debbie stirred and her eyelids fluttered open.

Simon came back into the room.

'They said to take her to the hospital now,' he said. They want to admit her just in case. I'll get the car out. Kids, you'll just have to . . .' His voice tailed away, and lines of worry creased his forehead.

Titus cleared his throat. Simon seemed to notice him for the first time.

'Don't worry about the children,' he said. 'They can come and stay next door tonight. Professor Tovey isn't home at the moment but I'm sure he would agree. Sarah will look after them.' He looked across at his sister, and she smiled and nodded her head. 'Tom can come with me to Meru tomorrow,' Titus went on. He smiled at Kelly-Ann. 'And your little friend too, of course.'

Tom said nothing. The sight of Mum lying there, unconscious and as white as a sheet, was paralysing him with fear. He felt he ought to offer to stay, to look after Bella and help Dad at home, but he couldn't bring out a single word.

'I don't know,' Simon was saying. He was holding a glass of water to Debbie's lips.

'I'll be all right,' she said weakly, struggling to sit up. The effort was too much. 'Oh dear, I think I'm going to faint again.'

Sarah swooped on Bella and picked her up in her capacious arms. Bella didn't struggle, but her thumb went into her mouth, and she looked uncertainly at Debbie.

'You'll come with me, darling,' said Sarah. 'We'll look after you, Afra and me. We'll make some cookies together.'

'Please, Mr Wilkinson,' said Titus. 'You must take your wife to the hospital. Don't worry about anything. I'll take very good care of Tom and Kelly-Ann. We'll be staying in a very good lodge in the game park, and Joseph will be with us too. It's only for one night. Then I'll bring them safely back again. Mrs Wilkinson will be better by then, I'm sure. Bella will be fine too. You can see that she and Sarah are old friends.'

Simon looked at Bella. She had started playing with the ends of the scarf that was tied round Sarah's head. His face cleared and he smiled.

'Yes,' he said, 'you're right. It's the best thing we can do. Get your things, kids. Tom, you get Bella's stuff together. I must get your mum to the hospital right away.'

3

ELEPHANT RAIDERS

No one talked much that evening. Afra played with Bella. Joseph went off silently to the little house he shared with his mother, behind the bungalow.

Tom went to bed early. He'd never slept in Afra's house before and he lay awake for hours, worrying about his mum, listening to the creaking of the corrugated iron roof as it cooled in the night air, and the scurrying of some little four-footed creatures chasing each other around on the top of the ceiling overhead.

He felt tired and heavy-eyed in the morning.

It was a long drive to Meru. No one talked much. Kelly-Ann sat in the front seat of Titus's jeep and tried to chatter to him. He smiled down at her from time to time, his understanding eyes taking in her restless hands and her cramped little shoulders, but he didn't encourage her to go on talking.

Joseph and Tom sat in the back. Joseph looked stonily out of the window, aloof and withdrawn. He hadn't spoken a word to Tom since the journey had begun. Tom felt awful. He'd hardly slept a wink all night.

I wish I hadn't said that to Mum, he kept thinking. What if something happens to her, or the baby? I'll feel it's all my fault. He stared unseeingly out over the farms and plantations along the road, worrying at a torn fingernail with his teeth.

Several hours had passed almost in silence when the radio in the front of the jeep crackled noisily. Titus picked up the handset and talked into it in Swahili. He listened for a moment, said a few terse words, and replaced it. He spoke over his shoulder to the boys in the back, raising his voice so that they could hear him over the loud roar of the engine.

'A problem. A major problem,' he said. 'A farmer came down with a message to the rangers' station this morning, from a village halfway up Mount Kenya. Sounds serious. Elephants are raiding the fields. They do it from time to time, but now there's a young rogue bull who is terrorizing the whole village. We'll have to go and talk to the people. Don't worry, we have plenty of time to get to Meru before nightfall.'

The word 'elephant' seemed to trigger something in Kelly-Ann.

'I just love elephants,' she said, looking winsomely up at Titus. 'I've got a piggy bank one.'

Tom looked sideways at Joseph, hoping to get

a sympathetic look, but Joseph went on staring out of the window.

'You like elephants?' said Titus absently. 'That's good.'

The jeep had been climbing steadily for some time now, and in spite of his sense of depression, Tom couldn't help looking out eagerly at the view. As the road twisted and turned, going up and up, he caught glimpses of a series of magnificent rocky peaks crowned with snow.

'That's the summit of Mount Kenya,' said Titus.

There was something solemn in his voice and Tom shivered. The mountain looked wild and remote, its jagged crags soaring out of a dark green collar of forest, its white crest dazzling against the deep blue sky. Elephants were in the forest, he knew that. Elephants and leopards and monkeys and who knew what other wild creatures? The thought of them began to lift him out of his miserable mood.

Titus grunted suddenly and braked as a man in a camouflage uniform and a smart green beret with a rifle slung over his shoulder stepped out into the road. He pulled the jeep up beside him and wound his window down. They talked in Swahili for a while, then Titus nodded towards the back of the Land Rover.

'Get in,' he said.

The ranger climbed into the rear seat, beside Tom and Joseph.

'*Jambo*,' he said politely to the boys, putting his rifle carefully down on the floor. He put his hand out to shake theirs. 'I am Daniel.'

Tom squashed himself into a corner to make room for him and shuffled his feet carefully out of the way of the long metal barrel that was pointing at his ankles.

'What happened at the village?' he said to Titus. 'Why do they want you to go there?'

'The village is very close to a forest where elephants are living,' began Titus. He had turned off the main road now and the jeep was bumping up a deeply rutted track between ragged thorny hedges. Over the top of them, Tom could just see tiny fields, some bare of plants, some already covered with freshly growing vegetables.

'Who does the land belong to? That's the question,' Titus went on. 'The farmers think they own it, of course, but the elephants – they think it's theirs.' He eased the jeep expertly round a tricky corner. 'It was all forest up here fifty years ago, before the whites came. They cleared the trees and made their farms. They used to have big elephant hunts and all their rich friends came out from Europe to kill elephants for fun.'

'That's so awful! It makes me boil over when I think of it,' burst out Tom.

'Those people have gone now,' Titus said peaceably. 'No one's allowed to hunt elephants like that any more.'

'Good,' said Tom. 'I hate hunters.'

'Well,' said Titus, 'there was good and bad in those days. It's not any better now. The hunters have gone but there are far more people now. Look at all these little farms everywhere. These are poor farmers. They split the land up between them when the whites left and brought all their families to live here. But the elephants, they're so clever, they know the hunters have gone. They remember that they used to live on this land and they want to have it back.'

Daniel leaned over the seat beside Tom.

'They're terrorizing the people here,' he said. 'They're attacking them and rooting up all their crops. And now there's this young bull. He's very wild. He's making everyone too much afraid.'

Tom felt a thrill of fear. He'd seen films of charging elephants. They'd been completely terrifying. He looked round in every direction, scanning as much of the countryside as he could see. Everything looked quiet, the little houses with their corrugated iron roofs and their vegetable patches quite peaceful under the afternoon sun. He could even see someone stretched out asleep under a tree, his hat pulled down to shade his face.

Then he thought of the rifle on the floor behind him.

33

'If the elephants were here first,' he said, 'you can't blame them for coming back, can you? You're not going to shoot them, are you?'

Titus laughed.

'No, of course not, Tom. I would never shoot an elephant unless I really had to. We've come to talk to the people, and see what's happening. We have to find out if we can help them in some way.'

Kelly-Ann was wriggling in her seat.

'Elephants don't attack people,' she said. 'They're really sweet and kind. I've seen them on a video.'

'They're not always sweet and kind,' said Titus. 'They can be very dangerous. In fact they're the most dangerous animals in Africa.'

'But . . .' began Kelly-Ann.

Her bossy little voice infuriated Tom.

'Titus knows a lot more about elephants than you do,' he said. He nearly added, *So you can just shut up and listen*, but he didn't want to get a frosty look from Joseph.

Kelly-Ann was silent for a moment, then she said, in a small voice, 'They wouldn't go for us, would they?'

Titus shook his head.

'No, no, don't worry,' he said. 'They only emerge from the forest when it's dark. It's still early. We'll leave here before night falls.'

'You mean we won't see them?' said Tom, half relieved and half disappointed.

'Not today, I don't think,' said Titus. 'I hope not. The elephants here are dangerous. But don't worry, Tom. Tomorrow you'll definitely see many of them, and from a safe place, I promise.'

The jeep lurched suddenly, crashing down into a deep pothole and startling a flock of long-tailed widow-birds, who took off from the side of the road where they'd been feeding and skimmed away over the ground, their tails floating out behind them like long black streamers.

'They should make a proper road here,' said Kelly-Ann, whose bounciness seemed to have returned. 'This one's a disgrace.'

For the first time that day, Joseph looked at Tom, and for a moment their eyes met in mutual exasperation. Then Joseph looked away.

'You're outside the city now,' he said. 'The people here are poor. Where can they find enough money to build a road?'

Kelly-Ann seemed about to answer, but the Land Rover was roaring up the last hillside, and the noise of the engine was drowning out every other sound. It pulled up at last under a tree at the bottom of a village which straggled away up the hill.

Daniel opened the door and jumped out. Tom climbed out more slowly. He felt stiff and cramped after the long drive.

It was still mid-afternoon, and the sun was well up in the sky, but the air at this high altitude was cool, and so clean and pure it seemed to Tom as if it came from another age, a time before cities and exhaust fumes and pollution had ever existed.

He filled his lungs and exhaled vigorously. The coolness and the air and the altitude exhilarated him. It was impossible to go on being miserable up here on the roof of the world.

The place was affecting Joseph too. For the first time that day he smiled.

'Look,' he said, pointing down into the valley.

Below them a great eagle was circling watchfully over the land, the sunlight glinting on its tawny feathers.

'I wish I could do that,' said Joseph enviously.

There were shouts from above and both boys looked up. People were running down the track towards them. They crowded round Titus, talking excitedly in Swahili, then fell back as a big man, wearing a red baseball cap, pushed his way through, holding out his hand to shake Titus's.

'You are welcome,' he said in English. 'I am Echessa, the headman. Thank you for coming. We have been waiting for you.'

Titus began to walk beside him up the narrow path between bare ploughed fields towards the village. The villagers were bombarding him with an excited commentary.

Tom looked round curiously. A cluster of small square mud houses, whitewashed and thatched with shaggy long grass, stood close together at the top of the rise, with rough ground in between them. Titus and Mr Echessa paused and looked out over the fields that surrounded the village.

'Which direction do the elephants come from?' asked Titus.

'From over there! Over there!' several people answered eagerly, pointing to the fringe of forest that edged the cleared land a few hundred metres from the village.

'They come in the evening,' one man said. He was wearing a big straw hat and he pushed it to the back of his head as he spoke. 'They are very clever.' He shook his head, almost admiringly. 'One of them stands close to our houses. Look, you can see here, the mark of his tusks by the door.'

Tom looked. A jagged gash had been ripped through the whitewashed wall, exposing the dried mud beneath.

'He waves his ears at us and screams,' the man went on, 'and if anyone comes out of his house, he will chase them and try to kill them. Then while he is keeping us in our homes, the older elephants go to our fields. They can peacefully eat all our crops. They know we cannot come out to drive them away.'

The door in the hut behind him opened, and a woman came out. Her worn face broke into a smile when she saw Titus and the uniformed ranger.

'You have come to help us!' she said. She looked round at her neighbours and clapped her hands, doing a little jig with her feet. 'You have come to protect us against the elephants!'

A little girl and an older girl in a ragged blue dress came out of the hut too and stood beside her. A baby crawled out after them. The baby caught sight of Tom and Kelly-Ann, stared at their unfamiliar white faces for a moment, his eyes round with fear, and began to cry. The older girl picked him up and bounced him on her hip, trying to silence him.

Their mother was still speaking eagerly to Titus.

'The elephants came again last night,' she said. 'They have destroyed my crop of maize.'

The villagers were standing round in a circle, listening and nodding their heads.

'They have trampled all our fields,' said an old man. 'We have planted, but it is the elephants who have harvested.'

The woman picked up the little girl who was clinging to her skirt.

'Tell me,' she said to Titus. 'How am I going to feed these children of mine?'

Titus shook his head.

'I wish I knew,' he said.

4

KAWIRA

Someone ran into a hut and fetched out a stool for Titus. He sat down, and the villagers, squatting or standing around him, went on pouring out their stories. They were speaking Swahili now.

The girl in the blue dress, the baby still on her hip, sidled round the edge of the crowd of villagers to where Joseph, Tom and Kelly-Ann were standing. She was barefoot, and her feet instinctively chose the smoothest places to walk on.

'*Jambo*,' she said shyly.

'*Jambo*,' said Tom diffidently. He could speak a few words of Swahili now, but he couldn't understand much.

The girl smiled.

'It is all right,' she said. 'I used to go to school. I can speak English. My name is Kawira.'

'I'm Tom,' said Tom. He pointed to Joseph and Kelly-Ann. 'Joseph,' he said. 'Kelly-Ann.'

Kelly-Ann had been frowning. Now she stared at Kawira, her head cocked defiantly to one side.

'The elephants didn't really trample all your fields, did they?' she said. 'I don't believe it.'

'Come, I will show you,' answered Kawira.

She led them out of the village through a gap between the huts. Tom stopped. They'd been standing in the shadows and he was dazzled by the brilliant afternoon light. In front of them was a square of bare red earth, one of a patchwork of little fields strewn with stones that stretched away to the edge of the forest. Vegetable plants had been growing in it but they had been trampled flat, some torn out of the ground, others completely crushed.

'Look, here is the mark of the elephant's foot,' said Kawira, pointing at a huge depression the size of a dinner plate in the ground. 'The elephants, they come together – five or six of them maybe.'

'What? Every night?' said Tom.

'No.' Kawira shook her head. 'If they came every night how could we try to grow any crops at all? They roam far and wide in the forest. You can hear them many times, making a sound like this.' She lowered her voice as far as it would go and growled. 'When they make these deep, deep sounds, they can hear each other from ten miles apart.'

'Ten miles? They must be louder than . . . than a bomb going off,' said Tom.

'No. Only they can hear these deepest sounds. They are too low for our human ears.'

'Ten miles!' Joseph was frowning in disbelief. 'They're as good as radio transmitters.'

'They can be so quiet too,' said Kawira. 'When they want to be silent they walk without any sound at all, on their toes.'

'An elephant on tiptoe?' scoffed Kelly-Ann. 'We've heard it all now.'

Kawira was looking down at the ground.

'Look!'

She darted on a little further, the baby bouncing unprotestingly in her arms. 'It's the elephant's . . .'

She paused, looking for the right word, and pointed down at the mound like a big loaf of brown bread on the ground.

'It's the elephant's dung,' said Joseph.

No one said anything for a moment. Tom looked round uneasily, half expecting an elephant to dash out of the forest and charge him at any second.

'Yeah, well, anyway,' said Kelly-Ann at last. 'It's their right, isn't it? This was their land in the old days. They were here first. Why should people come along and take the elephants' land and then make a fuss when they want it back?'

Kawira frowned at her, puzzled.

'I do not understand you,' she said. 'These are the fields of my family. My grandfather bought them from the government many years ago. I was born here.'

'No, but Kelly-Ann's got a point,' began Tom. 'I mean animals should have rights too, shouldn't they? The people here could move somewhere else, after all.'

Joseph, who had hardly said a word all day, suddenly exploded.

'It's so easy for you white people!' He bent down, picked up the tangled, broken stem of a plant and shook it in Tom's face. 'You don't understand anything, anything, of how it is to be poor in this country. What do you mean, the people can go somewhere else? Where can they go? This is their home! If someone comes to your house and says, "You must go, we want to pull down your house, you have no right to this piece of land because it's only for the animals", will you be happy?'

'Back off, Joseph,' said Tom, stepping away. 'I didn't mean—'

But the lid had come off Joseph's anger and nothing would stop it pouring out now.

'You people, what do you know? They are poor farmers here. The only thing they have is their land and their families. In Africa we love our land and we love our families.'

'Who do you think you are?' said Tom, beginning to feel unfairly attacked. 'We love our families just as much as you do.'

'No!' Joseph was glaring at him. 'You don't respect each other. You don't even love your own mother.'

'I do!' said Tom indignantly. 'I . . .'

He remembered the row he'd had with Debbie the night before and stopped.

'It is impossible for an African to speak to his mother in such a way as you did,' said Joseph haughtily.

Tom glared back at him, furious himself now.

'I didn't mean to. She'd been going on and on at me.'

'She's your mother! You have no respect!'

Tom wanted to punch him.

'Anyway, who do you think you are?' he yelled. 'You know it all, don't you! I'm rubbish, right? White people are all rubbish, are they? Africans are totally perfect, is that it?'

They stood face to face, balling their fists, conscious only of each other and the rage pumping round inside them.

After a moment, Joseph punched himself on the forehead with the palm of his hand.

'OK,' he said. 'OK, you're not rubbish. We're not perfect. I didn't mean to say it like that. But you're so lucky, Tom. You have a nice father and mother and a little sister – a real family. Sometimes I think you don't care about them at all. I just feel – I just wish I had a family like yours.'

He wrapped his arms round himself and turned away. Tom kicked at a stone with his foot. His anger had subsided too. Joseph had told him once that his father had been a hard, strict man who had often beaten him. One day, five years ago,

43

he'd gone off to look for work in Zambia. He'd never come back.

Tom felt bad.

'Yeah, well.' Tom paused and turned away. 'Look, if you really want to know, I feel awful about what I said to Mum. I never meant to. It just sort of came out.' He kicked at the stone again. It rolled unsatisfactorily a few metres away and stopped. 'What happens if something goes wrong with her or the baby?' he went on, his voice rising with anxiety. 'It'll all be because of me.'

Joseph turned to look at him, surprised and concerned. Then he shook his head vehemently.

'Nothing will go wrong,' he said. He paused, then he grinned. 'Anyway, what do you mean by suggesting that Africans aren't perfect? Of course we're perfect! I'm perfect, anyway.'

'Yeah,' said Tom. 'A perfect twit if you ask me.'

He put up his hand, palm out, towards Joseph. Joseph raised his and slapped Tom's, then they grabbed each others' arms and began to wrestle.

'I don't get it,' said Kelly-Ann, looking from one to the other and shaking her head. 'One minute you're about to beat each other's brains out and the next you're like blood brothers or something. What's going on?'

Kawira had been watching them with a puzzled look on her face, trying to follow their rapid English.

44

'Do you like to see animals?' she said to Kelly-Ann. 'There are some monkeys who are living nearby, in those big trees. We can go and see them. Perhaps they are there now.'

Kelly-Ann's face lit up.

'Monkeys? Oh, I love monkeys,' she said. 'They're adorable.'

The baby on Kawira's lap had been gazing at her uncertainly, but he was getting used to her white face now. He smiled at her suddenly and made a cooing noise. Kelly-Ann smiled back at him and he put his hands over his eyes and peeped through them shyly at her.

Kelly-Ann laughed.

'He's cute,' she said. 'What's his name?'

'Eliud,' said Kawira, setting off down the path towards the trees.

Kelly-Ann trotted after her.

'Does your mum often let you take him out like this?' she said.

Kawira didn't seem to understand.

'I have to look after him,' she said. 'My mother works on our farm.'

'What? You babysit all the time?' said Kelly-Ann. 'What about when you're at school?'

'We do not have a school here,' said Kawira shortly, scrambling up a bank ahead of Kelly-Ann.

Eliud had been sucking his thumb, but, jolted

by Kawira's climb, it fell out of his mouth. His face puckered.

'Look, he's going to cry,' said Kelly-Ann. 'My auntie's baby, he's always crying. He only shuts up if she puts him in front of the telly. He loves that. Especially cartoons. You should try that with him.'

'Telly?' said Kawira enquiringly.

'You know, television,' said Kelly-Ann.

Kawira laughed.

'There is no television here,' she said. 'There is no electricity.'

'Then you've never seen *Uptown*?' said Kelly-Ann. 'It's my favourite programme. It's sort of like a soap. It's so brilliant. There's this total geek called Terry and he's always doing these really weird things, like, I mean, putting Jasmine's sandals on the barbecue instead of the spare ribs.'

Behind her, Tom and Joseph were stuffing their hands into their mouths, trying not to laugh out loud.

'Bet Kawira thinks she's an alien from outer space,' said Tom between giggles.

They had reached the clump of trees now. Tom looked round. The sun was still high in the sky, but the harsh light of early afternoon had gone and the colours all around were deepening. The red earth of the fields was mellowing to terracotta, the green of the trees to a lush emerald. Above

46

them, the snows of Mount Kenya were dazzlingly white.

People were working in the fields nearby, their once brightly coloured clothes dulled with dust. A group of men were carrying branches out from the forest and piling them high on the corners of the field.

'What are they doing?' Tom asked Kawira.

'They will be making fires after darkness falls,' she said. 'Sometimes the fires can frighten the elephants away from their crops.'

There was a pattering sound overhead as a shower of leaves and twigs descended. The four of them looked up.

'The monkeys are there,' said Kawira, pointing up to the highest branches.

'I can't see any monkeys,' said Tom, squinting up into the tree.

It was difficult to make out anything because of the dazzling shafts of sunlight that glanced through the dancing leaves as the branches moved in the breeze. Then Kawira said softly, 'Look, they are there, on the highest branch.'

'Where? There isn't anything!' said Kelly-Ann, too loudly.

There was a rustle overhead and a barking noise as the monkeys took fright at the alien presence below them.

'There!' said Joseph, grabbing Kelly-Ann's arm and pointing upwards. 'Look! They're Syke's monkeys – very beautiful, with black faces. Up there on that branch.'

Tom craned his neck, peering upwards. A couple of twigs fell on his upturned face. He shook them off.

'Where? Where?' he said. 'Oh!'

A young monkey, bolder than the others, was running down the main trunk of the tree. He stopped on a branch and sat down, letting his long plumed tail hang over the edge. His black face, framed in a ruff of white fur, looked old, sad and infinitely wise. He sat astride the branch, his little ebony hands holding on to it, then threw back his head and yawned, showing them his sharp white teeth.

'He is trying to frighten us,' whispered Kawira.

'He's beautiful! Oh, he's so lovely,' breathed Kelly-Ann. 'I wish I could hold him.'

'He doesn't want anyone to hold him,' Tom whispered back crossly. 'He's wild and free and grown-up.'

The monkey began to clack his teeth, making a loud chattering noise. Answering cries came from the top of the tree.

'He's warning them,' said Joseph. 'They're clever, Syke's monkeys. They have different cries. One is for snakes. One is for birds of prey.'

'You mean like words?' Tom turned to him in astonishment.

'Yes, really, it's like words.'

'So he's telling him there's this crowd of amazing, brilliant people down here and they'd all better come and look?'

Kawira was still peering up to the top of the tree.

'There is a female there, with a baby,' she said.

'I just can't see them,' said Kelly-Ann irritably. 'I just can't pick them out. How do you do it?'

'We are used to them,' said Kawira simply. 'We know them. They live here.'

The monkey on the low branch began to scamper about, made anxious by the continued presence of the humans.

'Let's go,' said Tom. 'We don't want to stress them out.'

'Oh, just a bit longer, please,' said Kelly-Ann. 'I haven't seen the baby yet.'

'Come on,' said Tom. He tugged at her arm. He was uneasy but he wasn't sure why. For the past few minutes he'd had an odd feeling, as if they were being watched.

Then suddenly, from the forest edge a few hundred metres away, came a terrifying roaring scream. Kawira gasped and held Eliud closer to her chest. The others froze in terror.

'What is it?' said Kelly-Ann.

'Elephants!' shouted Joseph and Kawira together. 'Run!'

5

THE ELEPHANT CHARGE

For a moment Tom stood still, too scared and confused to run after the others. The terrible roaring scream burst out again, but it seemed to be all around, to fill the whole hillside. He couldn't tell where it was coming from. He wasn't sure if the others were running in the right direction. He didn't know which way to go.

Then he saw it. A huge elephant was breaking out from the edge of the forest, its big ears flapping, its trunk held high. In spite of its vast bulk it seemed almost light on its feet. It was charging straight towards the group of men near the edge of a field, but before it reached them it veered off. It was coming in his direction! It was making straight for him!

Adrenalin surged through him and he began to run, faster than he had ever run in his life before. The elephant was still a long way behind him but it was gaining on him fast. The air was full of its fearful trumpeting and he could hear its feet thundering on the ground. It was like the worst nightmare he had ever had. It was like being caught on a motorway with a ten-ton truck bearing down on him. It was like being stuck on a railway line in the path of an express train.

He raced on, bounding over the bare fields, stumbling over stones and low bushes. He wasn't far behind the others now. Joseph was miles ahead, with Kelly-Ann close behind, but Kawira, handicapped by the heavy baby in her arms, was slowing down.

He ran past her.

'Come on!' he shouted. 'It'll get you!'

He looked over his shoulder. The elephant was catching them up. He could see its tusks, long shafts of ivory, curling inwards a little at the tips. Its trunk was curled back against its forehead as if it was poised to strike a crushing blow.

Then, to his horror, he saw Kawira stumble and little Eliud fall out of her arms. As if in slow motion, he watched Kawira dive to pick him up, then fall over herself. They were both lying on the ground, right in the path of the charging elephant.

He hesitated for a terrible moment, knowing he ought to run back to help them, but then the elephant's petrifying scream of rage came again.

If I go back I'll only get killed too, he thought, and he ran on.

He wasn't far from the village now, but there was still a hundred metres or so of open ground to cover and he wasn't sure if he would make it. Then he saw a low hedge of bushes just over to his right, swerved, and dived down behind it. Joseph and Kelly-Ann were there already.

'Kawira fell over and dropped Eliud,' he gasped. 'I couldn't do anything. They were too far behind me.'

Kelly-Ann was deathly pale and trembling all over. She gasped and put her hand over her mouth. Joseph parted the bushes with great caution and looked out. Tom did the same.

Kawira was still on the ground, protecting Eliud with her body. The elephant had stopped a few yards away from them. He was flapping his ears, making the dust that covered them fly up into the air. His trunk was twirling about, and he stood above the girl and the baby at his full height, swinging his front legs to and fro as if he was deciding what to do.

'I can't look. I can't,' moaned Tom, covering his eyes.

Then he heard the pounding of gigantic feet again and a crashing, splintering noise. A sob rose in his throat. He was barely conscious of Kelly-Ann, who had grabbed hold of his arm and was crouching close to him, stunned, her mouth half open like a toddler gathering herself for a scream.

'It's all right, he isn't going for Kawira,' said Joseph, still looking out through the bushes.

Tom willed himself to look too. The elephant had turned aside from Kawira. He was venting his fury on a tree which grew in a corner between two fields. He was hacking at it with his tusks, leaning his trunk against it and pushing it with the whole weight of his body. The tree was giving way, the trunk splitting, the branches crashing down to the earth. Now the elephant was tearing ragged trunkfuls of leaves away and tossing them to the wind. The sound of the breaking wood, the smashing and splintering, were almost as frightening as the trumpeting itself.

With his heart in his mouth, Tom watched as Kawira struggled to her feet, picked up Eliud, who was crying at the top of his voice, and raced towards the village, disappearing a few moments later between the low thatched huts.

'We must go. We can't stay here,' Joseph whispered.

'But he'll see us,' responded Tom urgently. 'He'll get us before we get to the houses.'

'Yes, you're right. He's trying to find us now. Look,' whispered Joseph. 'We must be very quiet. Elephants can hear everything. They can hear a person talking from two miles away.'

'I'm scared! I don't want to stay here!' moaned Kelly-Ann.

'Be quiet!'

'Shut up!' Both boys turned on her with frantic whispers. 'Do you want him to get us?'

Kelly-Ann subsided for a moment, then gave a little scream.

'Titus!' she called out. 'Here! We're here! Help!'

Titus was running out of the village towards them with Daniel beside him. Daniel was holding his gun to his shoulder, as if ready to shoot. Kelly-Ann stood up and began to stumble towards them, sobbing loudly.

'Help me!' she was crying. 'Don't let it get me! Send it away!'

Titus raced towards her, grabbed her in his arms and ran with her back to the shelter of the village. The elephant, who had finished demolishing the tree, raised his head, ignoring Titus but watching Daniel who was advancing cautiously towards him.

Titus appeared again.

'Tom! Joseph! Where are you?' he called. 'Come! Daniel will cover you. Get back to the village. Walk slowly. Don't run. Don't panic him or we'll have to shoot him.'

The boys stood up. The bushes, flimsy as they were, now seemed like a safe haven to Tom, and the open ground between him and the village like an endless plain, a no man's land, a mile-long expanse of terror.

'That's right, walk slowly,' Titus was calling to them in a calm voice. 'Don't look round at him. He's quiet. He's not bothering about you.'

In spite of himself, Tom could not resist looking over his shoulder. The elephant had advanced a few paces towards them. He seemed to be watching, unsure of what to do. He was rocking

54

from side to side and blowing air violently out of his trunk.

Then, from the corner of his eyes, Tom saw one of the farmers who had been collecting wood break from the cover where he had been hiding and make a dash for the village. The elephant saw him and reacted as if he'd been stung. With a piercing roar he charged at the man, his ears flapping wildly, his trunk outstretched.

Daniel stopped advancing and took aim down the sights of his gun. Tom, suddenly weak with relief, raced over the last few metres to the sheltering walls of the village where the people were huddled in fear, and turned to watch.

The elephant was terrifying in his rage, but his power was magnificent. He was running at full speed, his great muscles rippling under his wrinkled skin, his huge head tossing up and down.

In spite of his fear, Tom couldn't bear the idea of him crashing down, felled by a bullet shot from an enemy he would never see, dying a death he would never understand.

Don't shoot, don't shoot, he pleaded with Daniel under his breath. 'Run, run!' he heard himself shouting out loud to the farmer.

The farmer had reached a steep bank. He dived down it out of sight of the crowd of people who were standing all around Tom now. The elephant skidded to a halt and stood for a long moment while his anger appeared to die out in him. Slowly, his great ears subsided till they lay flat against his head, and his trunk relaxed. With a final defiant swing he coiled his trunk round a low bush, tore it up by the roots and tossed it over his shoulder. Then he turned and, with infinite dignity, he began to walk back towards the forest, giving out a low rumbling noise which echoed round the empty hillside like the purr of a huge engine.

Everyone had been holding their breath but now they all started talking at once. The villagers were surrounding Titus, arguing vociferously with him in Swahili. Kawira was sobbing with relief and clinging to her mother who was anxiously examining Eliud for cuts and bruises and trying to comfort Kawira at the same time. Daniel was fending off a crowd of farmers who seemed to be angry with him for not shooting the elephant while he had the chance.

Tom felt too shaky to talk to anyone. His knees were weak and his heart was still pumping uncomfortably. He crept into a shady corner in the angle of two houses, sat down on a big stone and put his head down in his hands.

He couldn't get out of his mind the picture of Kawira diving down to rescue Eliud, then trying to protect him from the raging elephant with her own body. It was the bravest thing he'd ever seen in his life. A picture of Mum and the new baby floated into his mind, and he shuddered.

I should have gone back, he kept thinking. I should have tried to help them.

Someone nudged him. He looked up. Joseph was beside him, pointing to Kelly-Ann who was wandering through the crowd of people, her pink dress dirty and crumpled, her hair tangled, her face streaked with tears.

'Tom!' she was shouting. 'Where are you? Tom?'

Tom groaned. He didn't want to cope with Kelly-Ann at the moment, but he lifted his hand and waved to her. She ran over to him. She looked scrawny and pathetic and suddenly he felt sorry for her.

'We've got to get out of here,' she said. 'It might come back. Titus promised your dad he'd get us to Meru. Tell him we want to go now.'

'It's not like that, Kelly-Ann,' said Tom. 'What about the people here? Titus can't just leave them. He's come here to help them.'

'But he promised,' wailed Kelly-Ann. 'It's not fair! He shouldn't have brought us here. We should never have left Nairobi. I wish I'd gone to the coast with Mum.'

'Well, why didn't you then?' demanded Tom.

Kelly-Ann's woebegone face slumped even further and her eyes filled again.

'Because my mum's boyfriend didn't want me to, that's why.'

'Oh,' said Tom. 'I see.' He stood up. He felt he

ought to cheer her up but he didn't know how. 'Yeah well, anyway, look on the bright side. I mean the elephant didn't get you, did he, and you'll have a brilliant story to tell your mum.'

Titus came over to them.

'Tom, Kelly-Ann, are you all right? I was very worried about you all when I heard the elephant trumpeting. It's very unusual, the people here have been telling me, for an elephant to come out so early in the afternoon. Daniel had the chance to examine him through his binoculars. Did you see that he has a wound at the side of his head? It's just near his eye – a sensitive place. It doesn't appear to be infected, but he's probably experiencing great pain. It isn't surprising that his temper's bad.'

'Will you have to shoot him?' said Tom.

'Maybe. I don't know yet. His wound will soon heal and his temper will improve. But if he continues to terrorize people, we'll have to do it.'

Kelly-Ann sniffed dolefully.

'Please, Titus,' she said in a little-girly voice that set Tom's teeth on edge. 'Can we go now?'

'Yes. It's time to go.'

Titus waved to Daniel and they all began to walk back towards the jeep which was parked on the far side of the village. 'I'll return tomorrow to discuss the matter with the people here, but you don't have to come with me if you don't wish to.'

They had reached the jeep now and climbed in; Tom, Joseph and Kelly-Ann in the back and Daniel in the front beside Titus. Kawira ran up to them and stood beside the window.

'Goodbye,' she said shyly. 'I hope we meet again one day.'

Titus started the engine and the jeep began to move off down the track.

'Mr Musau! Look!' Daniel suddenly called out urgently.

'What is it?' said Titus.

'Look there!' said Daniel. 'On the next bend, further down the track. Elephants! We had better turn back to the village.'

They all peered forward and out through the windscreen. Tom couldn't see anything at first except for a clump of trees. Then he realized that what he'd thought was a patch of shade was a huge dark body, and the long protruberance that had been waving slowly like a branch in the breeze was a trunk.

The elephant stepped slowly out into the road, and another followed. They were feeling around on the ground with their trunks with extraordinary delicacy, picking up the small pods that had fallen from the trees and transferring them to their mouths.

'Do you see that?' said Titus. 'The tips of their trunks are as delicate as our fingers. I heard of an elephant once who could pick up a pin.'

He put the jeep into reverse and began to back cautiously away.

'Can't we drive round them?' said Kelly-Ann. 'How are we going to get away from here?'

'It's too late to get away,' said Titus. 'We have no choice. We're staying for the night.'

6

TUSK ATTACK!

A spasm of fear gripped Tom's stomach. He hadn't realized until that moment how relieved he'd been at the thought of leaving the village behind him. He waited for an explosion from Kelly-Ann but to his surprise it didn't come. She was sitting between him and Joseph in the back of the jeep. He looked down at her. Her face was flushed and her lips tightly pursed. She looked more angry than scared.

It was Joseph who spoke, but in Swahili. He seemed to be arguing with Titus. Daniel in the front seat turned at last and said in English, 'Do not be afraid, Joseph. I have my rifle. If it is necessary we will know how to protect you.'

Joseph sat back, looking embarrassed.

He's scared too, Tom thought with relief.

They had reversed back up to the village now. The crowd that had come to see them off had dispersed and only a couple of women remained. They carried plastic jerrycans in their hands and they were walking across an open space at the bottom of the village to where a stand pipe with a tap on it stood out from a concrete platform.

They called out a question, and Titus leaned out of the window of the jeep and answered them. The women looked nervously past him down the road.

Daniel called out something else, and the women began to run towards the stand pipe.

'What did he say?' Tom asked Joseph.

'He says the elephants are still quite far off,' answered Joseph. 'The women will have time to fetch their water if they hurry.'

His voice shook a little. Titus turned off the ignition. 'Listen, all of you. Don't be afraid. These are very kind people here. They'll look after us. We'll be safe here with them.'

They all climbed out of the jeep and stood beside it for a moment, not knowing what to do. Then Kawira appeared, smiling with delight.

'You have come back! Did you leave something behind?'

'No,' said Tom. 'There are elephants on the track.'

'He says we've got to stay,' Kelly-Ann said furiously, staring at Titus's broad back. 'It's outrageous. We're supposed to be in that nice hotel in Meru. I'm going to tell Simon about this. It's completely out of order. I just don't believe this is happening to me.'

'You will stay here tonight?' said Kawira, who had been following Kelly-Ann with difficulty. 'You can stay with us! I will ask my mother.'

She stopped and her face clouded over. Then she turned to Joseph and said something in Swahili.

'What's she saying?' demanded Kelly-Ann.

Joseph was looking at the ground, his face wooden.

'She says they're poor people and they don't have a very comfortable house. But you're very welcome to whatever they have.'

Kelly-Ann opened her mouth but Tom jumped in before she could say anything.

'Thanks, Kawira,' he said. 'We'll ask Titus. We'd like to stay with you if he says we can.'

Titus and Daniel were unloading bags from the back of the jeep. A crowd had gathered by now. Everyone was pressing them to stay. Mr Echessa, the man with the red baseball cap, approached. People parted to let him through.

'Here is our headman,' Kawira said, disappointed. 'He will ask you to be his guests. You must go with him.'

Mr Echessa talked briefly to Titus then began to walk with him up to a new house, bigger than the rest, which stood within an enclosure of thorns at the highest point of the village. Titus looked back and signalled to Tom and the others.

'We'll stay in Mr Echessa's house tonight,' he called out to them.

The old man smiled at them.

'You're welcome!' he said, his lined and

weathered face relaxing into a broad smile. 'We'll kill a goat for you.'

Tom looked at Kelly-Ann. Luckily she hadn't heard. She was staring beyond the crowd at two women who were running into the village. Tom recognized them at once. They were the same women who had been on their way to the stand pipe for water an hour earlier. They weren't carrying their jerrycans now.

'*Ndovo! Ndovo!*' the women were shouting.

'*Ndovo*? That means elephant,' gasped Tom.

Titus turned round. He was some way up the path now.

'Come here, all of you, quickly!' he yelled at them.

Everyone was scattering into their houses. Kawira grabbed Tom's hand.

'My house is just here,' she said. 'Come!'

Tom looked up towards Titus, but at that moment he heard people screaming in the distance. Kawira tugged at his hand again and he dashed after her with Joseph and Kelly-Ann in his wake. A moment later they were inside Kawira's house and the door was shut behind them.

It was so dark in the little house that at first Tom couldn't see anything at all. Then he caught the acrid smell of a wood fire and saw the faint glow of burning embers. After a moment, as his eyes adjusted, he began to make out more and more in the faint light that penetrated the gap round the loosely fitting door.

He felt safe for the moment. He could hear nothing from outside, no more trumpeting, no heavy feet pounding the earth. He listened, every nerve quivering, but there was no sound at all from outside. He let out his breath in relief.

He peered curiously round the little house. There was only one room. Against one wall he could make out the shape of a wooden bed frame, with several metal suitcases piled beside it. A fire, mainly consisting of a heap of white ashes, burned dully in the middle of the mud floor of the room, the smoke coiling up to escape through the thatched roof above.

Kawira's mother had been sitting by the fire breastfeeding a sleepy Eliud, but she jumped to her feet when her visitors burst in.

'*Ndovo!*' cried Kawira. 'The elephants are coming!'

Her mother put her hand up to her mouth and ran to the door. She peered through the crack, then turned back and looked distractedly at Kelly-Ann and the boys.

'I am happy to see you,' she said. Then her voice dropped almost to a whisper. 'But please, you must not make any noise. The elephants maybe are not far from here. If they hear us, they will crush our house.'

Kawira took out a straw mat that had been rolled up by the wall and spread it out by the fire.

'Come, sit down,' she whispered.

Kelly-Ann plumped herself down on the mat, and Kawira sat down beside her. Joseph had already crouched down by the door, his back against the wall, as if poised to leap up at any moment. Tom sat down beside him. There was a long crack by the door where the post had worked a little loose from the dry mud wall, and through it he could see a thin sliver of the outside world.

He could sense Joseph beside him, his body as taut as a hunted hare. He looked across at Kelly-Ann and Kawira. Kawira's big eyes were turned apprehensively towards her mother. Her little sister, who had been playing quietly by a row of big earthenware jars in the corner, ran over to her mother and buried her head in her lap.

'I can't hear anything,' Tom whispered tentatively. 'Maybe there's nothing out there after all. Maybe it would be safe to go out and look for Titus and the rangers.'

'It's not safe! Elephants can move as silently as mice,' Joseph whispered back, so quietly he was barely audible. 'We won't hear them if they don't want us to.'

'But why would they come into the village?' persisted Tom.

Kawira leaned forward.

'Didn't Mr Musau tell you before? The elephants send one of them to guard the village while the others go to the fields.'

The light outside was fading rapidly as evening fell and it was getting harder to make out anything inside the house, but in the dim firelight Tom could see Kawira's mother rocking backwards and forwards on her low stool, tears running down her cheeks.

For the first time that day, Kelly-Ann seemed to be silenced. She sat quietly, watching Kawira's mother who was cradling Eliud in her arms.

Then, from outside, came the sound that Tom had been dreading – a deep rolling rumble, close by.

Tom twisted his head round and looked out through the crack. The earlier glimpse of a section of the hut on the other side of the piece of dusty ground was obscured now by a grey wall, a moving, leathery hide, wrinkled and caked with flakes of dried mud. It was so close that if he'd put his arm out through the crack in the wall he could almost have touched it.

There was a moment of silence and the great grey body was still. Tom was holding his breath. It was building up inside him till he felt he would burst, but he didn't dare let it go in case he made a noise. Then, as if the elephant had made up its mind, the huge bulk moved round so that it was no longer standing sideways to the house. For a moment, Tom saw daylight again and the reassuring view of huts across the village, but an instant later there was a confused jumble of grey and white, a flapping ear, a long flash of ivory, and his heart bounded with pure terror as the elephant ran his tusks into the house, shaking it to its rickety foundations.

Tom couldn't bear to look any longer. He turned his head away. He hardly felt Joseph's hand which had closed like a vice on his wrist. His whole body was rigid with tension. He was afraid he would faint. He looked round wildly, hoping to see a hole somewhere in the far wall through which he could escape, then he caught a signal from Kawira's mother. She was leaning forward on her stool, locking eyes in turn with each of the children as if she was willing them to be silent.

The thudding sound came again, and again the whole house shook. Panic had seized Tom. It was squeezing him by the throat, throttling him. He could hear a loud flapping sound now, like a canvas sail blowing backwards and forwards in the wind.

The elephant's flapping his ears, he thought. He's going to go for us, like he went for that tree. He's going to knock the whole house down and gore and trample us all to death.

7

RESCUE

Tom's heart was thudding so loudly in his ears it sounded like a drumbeat, and he was almost afraid that the elephant would hear it and be maddened still further. He sat with his arms round his knees, gripping them so tightly that all his muscles ached. Beside him, Joseph sat with his head hunched down into his shoulders, his lips moving silently as if he was praying.

Kelly-Ann had let out a whimper at the first strike of the elephant's tusks, but Kawira's mother had urgently gestured her to be silent. Now Kawira reached out for her and put her trembling arms round her. Kelly-Ann seemed to crumple inside, then she turned and clung to Kawira, burying her head in Kawira's shoulder.

The tension grew. Another terrible blow shook the roof and sections of mud wall fell away into the house, landing in a shower of dusty crumbs on the floor.

Tom had to hold himself down. The urge to jump up and shout, to break out of the house and run was almost stronger than he could bear.

Then suddenly the thudding blows stopped.

There were confused sounds from some way away. People were shouting. Shots were being fired.

The elephant trumpeted, a wild, furious scream that shook the flimsy little house from top to bottom and turned Tom's bones to water. There was the sound of heavy feet going away, and after that, silence.

A few moments later, the door burst open and Titus rushed in.

'Oh thank God, you're safe!' he said, his usually deep voice high with anxiety.

'Has it gone? Have all the elephants gone? Did you shoot at them?' demanded Joseph, turning his strained face up to his uncle.

'Daniel's dealing with them now. They're retreating.' Titus dropped down onto his haunches beside Joseph and squeezed his shoulders. 'I was so worried about you! I didn't see where you'd gone. Daniel and I were running from house to house looking for you and someone told us you were in the very house the elephant was attacking. We came up behind the elephant and shot over his head. He was frightened and ran off. Daniel's out there now with the farmers. They've started their fires and they're making a big noise to drive all the elephants away. Listen.'

He put up his hand. Tom listened. He could hear men's voices shouting and the sound of metal objects banging together in the distance. He dropped his head onto his knees. He was weak with relief and shaking uncontrollably.

Titus looked enquiringly up at Kawira's mother. 'Thank you, Mrs . . .'

'Grace,' she said. 'My name is Grace.'

She stood up and laid Eliud, who had amazingly fallen asleep, on the bed.

'You see how it is with us,' she said.

The quiet despair in her voice made Tom look up. The faint glow of the fire cast a bronze light on her strong face.

Mum would go crazy if it was her, he thought.

Grace crouched down beside her little girl who was still holding on to her skirt, still terrified into silence.

'Come, Susanna,' she said, picking her up. She looked over the child's head to Titus. 'We cannot go on living in this way. You must help us.'

'Your husband,' Titus said tentatively. 'He's not here?'

'My husband died last year,' said Grace. 'He was a wildlife guide for tourists. There was an accident. The Land Rover turned over.'

Titus shook his head and sucked in his breath sympathetically. Then he cleared his throat.

'Come with me up to Mr Echessa's house,' he said. 'We'll discuss all these matters there. And if the elephants return you'll be safer up there than you are here.'

Kelly-Ann had begun to cry loudly with

childish sniffs and hiccups. She was still clinging to Kawira like a bean to a pole, as if she had suddenly decided that Kawira was her best friend.

Tom moved away from her. He wanted to do something drastic for this family, to summon a millionaire to whisk them away to a safe comfortable place, to make himself into a wizard and touch everything they had and turn it to gold.

'I want my friend to come too,' said Kelly-Ann babyishly, looking at Titus.

'We're all going.' At last Titus allowed a hint of impatience to colour his voice. 'Look at Susanna. She's only a baby but she's braver than you. Come, let's go. It's safe now. Daniel and the farmers are keeping the elephants away. Mr Echessa's waiting at his house for us.'

He went out, ducking his head under the low doorway. Tom didn't wait any longer. He was dying to get out of the little house, to see for himself what was going on outside. He and Joseph moved together, collided in the narrow doorway, and burst out through it like a couple of peas exploding from a pod.

They could hear shouting from below the village and slipped behind Grace's little house to look out over the fields. Fires had been lit in several places, and silhouetted against the brilliant orange flames they could see the figures of men and boys piling on more wood and banging metal strips together. Daniel was standing quietly beside them, his rifle at the ready in his hand. There was no sign of the elephants.

'They've gone back to the forest then,' said Tom, coughing a bit to hide the fact that his voice was still shaking.

'Boys! Come!' Titus's voice floated back to them. 'We must stay together now.'

They set off behind him up the short hill towards the big house at the top of the village. Kawira, with Eliud in her arms and Kelly-Ann glued to her side, walked beside Titus, and Grace, hampered by the dead weight of Susanna, was trying to padlock the door of her little house.

Tom suddenly thought of Mum and Bella. He'd often seen Debbie awkwardly trying to open a drawer, or turn a handle, or pick something up from the floor, with Bella in her arms. It hadn't often occurred to him to help her.

He ran up to Grace.

'Here, I'll do it,' he said shyly.

Grace smiled at him and dropped the padlock into his hand, then bent down to pick up the bag she had brought out with her.

'It's OK, I'll carry it,' said Tom, quickly closing the padlock and handing her back the key.

There was no moon, and the only light came from the stars and the gleam of the few kerosene lamps through the open doors of some of the village houses. Tom and Joseph stayed close to

Grace who knew every bump and hollow in the ground of the village's central space.

Neither of them spoke. Tom's senses were still tinglingly alert. His eyes strained to pierce the darkness, where every dim shape looked menacing. His ears were pricked to hear beyond the shouts of the men in the field. He was listening to the forest, for wild sounds from wild things. Once he thought he heard a leopard cough and he halted suddenly, so that Grace's heavy bag banged into the side of his leg. Then he realized it was only a dog barking.

They were near the headman's house now. The door was open and light streamed out. In the doorway, Tom could see Kawira and Kelly-Ann. Kawira was holding Eliud up to an older woman who was taking him out of her arms. Kawira's supple back was arched. Her head, capped with its crown of soft black hair, was tilted to one side.

She's like a . . . like a . . . He hunted around in his mind for a comparison and thought suddenly of a graceful little antelope he'd seen a few weeks ago, reaching up to nibble fresh young leaves from a tree.

That's silly, he told himself. A girl can't be like an antelope. But the idea pleased him all the same.

As he watched, Kelly-Ann put her arm possessively through Kawira's and they went into the house, out of sight. Tom nearly stumbled over a stone.

'I don't care what you think,' he said to Joseph, 'but Kelly-Ann's driving me round the twist. I want to murder her.'

In the dark beside him, he sensed that Joseph was grinning.

'You'd better hurry up and murder her soon, then,' he said, 'in case I do it first.'

8

MR ECHESSA'S HOUSE

An eerie sound in the distance made Tom and Joseph stop just outside Mr Echessa's house. They turned simultaneously and looked back down the hill. In the fields below, they could see the dancing flames of the fires. The men's voices, rising and falling in the musical rhythms of Swahili, floated up to them through the silent night air.

The strange sound came again.

'Hyenas,' said Tom, trying to sound as if he really knew and looking beyond the fires to the dark swathe of forest beyond.

Joseph shuddered, but said nothing.

'You don't think it's something – you know – weird, do you?' said Tom, who had often heard Joseph retell stories of the ghosts and spirits his grandfather had seen as a boy.

Joseph didn't answer, but hurried on into the house. Tom shivered.

I'm just cold, he told himself.

Now that he thought about it, he realized that he really was cold. A breeze had sprung up, whistling down from the freezing summit of the mountain. It penetrated his light shirt and shorts and whipped round his bare arms and legs.

He took one last look at the dark forest, then hurried inside after Joseph.

Mr Echessa's house was full of light that streamed from a kerosene lamp set on a low table, and Tom, whose eyes were used to the dark, blinked rapidly as they adjusted.

The room was crowded with people. The older men were sitting on armchairs arranged around the walls, while the younger ones squatted beside them, or sat cross-legged on mats at their feet. A curtain divided the room and from behind it he could hear Eliud's babyish gurgling, and women's voices, and the clatter of pots and pans as if a meal was being prepared.

Titus was sitting in one of the armchairs next to Mr Echessa. He saw the two boys hesitating by the door and beckoned to them.

'You can sit here,' he said, pointing to the cowskin mat by his feet.

They went over and sat down. The conversation in Swahili bubbled along over Tom's head. He could understand the occasional word, but he couldn't make out what they were talking about. He soon gave up trying to follow. His stomach was rumbling. He realized he was hungry.

After a while, people began to stand up and say goodbye, shaking hands with Titus and clapping the boys on their shoulders as they went past.

'Come,' said Mr Echessa jovially, patting a now empty armchair beside him. 'Sit here, Tom, and you, Joseph, go beside your uncle. You have experienced our elephants today. You see how it is for us.'

'I've never been so scared in my whole life,' said Tom, shuddering.

'I thought we were going to die,' said Joseph.

Kelly-Ann came forward, dragging Kawira, who seemed overcome by shyness in the presence of the headman. She pushed Kawira into another chair and plumped herself down beside Tom.

'I mean it was totally unbelievable,' she began. She opened her eyes wide at Mr Echessa, wanting to impress him. 'We were trembling so much I thought we'd shake ourselves to bits. We were, weren't we, Kawira?'

Tom caught Kawira's eye, raised his eyebrows towards Kelly-Ann and shook his head with a grimace. Kawira recovered momentarily from her embarrassment and gave him a sudden flashing smile.

'Yes, we were very frightened,' she said.

'You see?' said Mr Echessa, turning to Titus. His smile had dropped away and he leaned forward in his chair. 'It is as I keep telling you. Even our children are frightened. We must have protection. What will you do to help us?'

Titus cleared his throat and shifted in his seat.

'It's a very difficult problem,' he began.

'What about an electric fence, Uncle Titus?' said Joseph. 'They have them in some places, don't they? Couldn't you put one here, to keep the elephants away from the fields?'

Titus nodded slowly.

'It's sometimes possible, yes,' he said. 'But think how long the fence would have to be. It would be very expensive to build.'

'And there isn't any electricity here,' put in Tom.

'Oh that's not a problem.' Joseph was frowning, thinking things through. 'Fences can be solar-powered. You put solar panels near them and they get plenty of electricity that way.'

'That's brilliant,' said Tom, impressed. 'That's the answer then, isn't it? Electric fences?'

Titus tilted his head doubtfully to one side.

'It's not so easy,' he said. 'Elephants are very determined. They learn how to break the electric fences. At first they're frightened of them and they stay away, but they soon discover that if they touch the wires only with their tusks the electricity doesn't hurt them.'

'But they couldn't pull a big fence down just with their tusks, could they?' objected Tom.

'That's what they try to do at first. If they don't succeed, they root around at the base of the fence posts until they're loose, then they push them over.'

'Make the posts stronger then,' said Tom.

'An elephant can knock down even a big tree,' said Kawira softly. 'You could not find a post strong enough to stop them.'

'And even if they can't knock down the posts,' Titus went on, 'if they really want to break through a fence, they'll choose one of their number, a volunteer, just like we might do, and he or she will charge at the fence and accept the pain of the shock until they've broken it down.'

Tom whistled.

'That's incredible,' he said.

'Elephants are incredible animals. I could tell you so many stories, of their courage, their intelligence, their loyalty. Did you know that they actually bury their dead?'

'What?' Tom looked disbelievingly at him.

Titus smiled at him.

'I've seen it with my own eyes. When they find elephant bones they examine them carefully, especially the tusks. Then they cover them over with heaps of dead leaves and branches.'

'That's incredible,' said Tom. 'They're kind of like people.'

'But don't forget their great destructiveness,' said Mr Echessa sharply, who didn't seem to like the way the conversation was going.

'Do you want the rangers to shoot them then?' Tom asked him.

Mr Echessa paused, and even little Eliud, who

had woken up now and was squealing noisily, quietened down as if waiting for his answer.

'Yes,' Mr Echessa said at last. 'When they get the habit of terrorizing us, then yes, we want to shoot them. But Mr Musau is right. They're noble animals. We don't want to exterminate them or harm them in any way. In the past we've always lived peacefully with elephants. But we don't want them right here, taking all our food from us. We just want them to go far away from our homes and our farms.'

'Then they'll go to where there are other farms,' said Titus, shaking his head. 'Everywhere in this country of ours, everywhere in Africa, the people are moving on to new lands, where the elephants once lived. Where can the elephants go?'

The curtain twitched again and Mr Echessa's wife appeared with Grace beside her. They were carrying steaming bowls of food that smelt delicious. Tom's mouth watered.

'We will think about all these problems later,' said Mr Echessa, rubbing his hands. 'Now, let's eat.'

The small table was soon covered in plates and glasses, spoons, forks and plates of food. Mrs Echessa began hospitably piling meat and something that looked like mashed potato onto the plates. She passed one to Tom and another to Kelly-Ann.

Kelly-Ann looked at the meat on the plate, then looked up at Mrs Echessa.

'I'm veg—' she began.

Tom glared at her.

'Just take it,' he hissed. 'You can give the meat to me later.'

Kelly-Ann took the plate from Mrs Echessa's hands and turned to stare at Tom, offended.

'What's the matter with you?' she said.

'They've made all this specially for us,' said Tom. 'They killed their goat to give us meat. It's the best thing they have. You can't just refuse to take it.'

'I'm not going to eat any meat,' said Kelly-Ann too loudly. 'It's disgusting.'

'Sh!' whispered Tom furiously. 'Here, shovel it onto my plate. There, now you can just eat the veg bits.'

Kelly-Ann put her fork into the mash on her plate and lifted a tiny bit to her mouth. Her eyebrows shot up in surprise.

'This is lovely,' she said to Kawira, who was helping Mrs Echessa pour out sodas into the glasses. 'What is it?'

'It is maize and beans and potatoes,' said Kawira. 'It is our food. Do you like it?'

'Yes, I really do,' said Kelly-Ann, settling into her chair to eat.

It was amazing, thought Tom, after he'd cleaned up every scrap of food on his plate, how much better you felt when you weren't hungry any more. Here in this cosy little house the terrors of the night outside seemed far away. It was incredible that only a few hours earlier they had been cowering, petrified, while an enraged elephant tried to break down the little house they were sheltering in.

'Where are we going to sleep?' said Kelly-Ann, nudging him suddenly with her sharp little elbow. 'I looked behind that curtain. There's no other rooms. No bedrooms or anything.'

'Wait and see what the others do,' said Tom, trying not to show that he was wondering himself.

There was a noise outside the door, the latch lifted and Daniel came in, carrying the bags from the jeep. He said something in Swahili to Titus, saluted, turned smartly and went outside again.

'What's happening?' said Tom. 'Have the elephants really gone?'

Titus nodded.

'For now, yes. The farmers have heard them moving away along the ridge. They do not think they will return tonight.'

'Where's Daniel going to sleep?' said Tom.

'He has a relative here in the village,' said Titus. 'He'll stay with him in his house.'

Grace stood up.

'*Asante sana*,' she said to Mrs Echessa. 'Thank you very much. We can return to our own house now.' She picked up Eliud and took Susanna's hand. 'Come, Kawira,' she said.

Kelly-Ann ran over to Kawira and grabbed her arm.

'Oh no, please don't go. Please, can she stay?' She looked from Grace to Mr Echessa. 'Let her stay the night.'

Mr Echessa laughed.

'You're friends with each other. That's very nice. Yes, she can stay here.'

Kawira looked anxiously at her mother. Grace gave a tiny nod. Reluctantly, Kawira sank down again onto her chair, and sat awkwardly on the edge of it watching her mother go.

Joseph went over to his bag, opened it and pulled out a sweater. Tom followed him. He took out a sweatshirt and a pair of warm tracksuit trousers from his own bag, looked doubtfully down at the pyjamas he'd packed, and shut his bag again. It was too cold to change into night things. He'd sleep in his clothes tonight.

Mrs Echessa had lifted a pile of mats and blankets down from a shelf inside the curtain, and was laying them out on the floor.

Titus looked at Tom.

'Will it be hard for you on the floor?' he said. 'Have you slept on a mat before? Without a mattress?'

'Yes,' lied Tom. 'Lots of times. I'll be fine.'

He lay down on a cowskin mat beside Joseph

and pulled a blanket over both of them. Kelly-Ann was still fussing over her things, putting on socks and taking slides out of her hair. She pattered over to another mat and sat down on it.

'Come on, Kawira,' she said. 'I don't suppose I'll sleep a wink – it's so hard on the floor. But we'll be together anyway, won't we?'

She giggled uncertainly.

Tom suddenly felt sleepy. He saw Kawira slip across to Kelly-Ann's mat and lie down beside her, then watched her carefully arrange the blanket around Kelly-Ann's taut little shoulders. But his eyes had closed before Kelly-Ann had finished fussily settling down, and long before the adults had made themselves ready for bed and put out the lamp, he was fast asleep.

9

THE POOL IN THE FOREST

Tom woke with a start in the middle of the night. He lay still for a moment, not knowing where he was, then felt an ache in his right hip and shoulder where they had been pressing on the unyielding floor, and turned over onto his back.

Everything came back in a rush. He could hear snores nearby, the deep throaty snores of a man – Mr Echessa or Titus, he supposed. Nearer to him someone was making whimpering, snuffling noises, like a puppy having a bad dream. He guessed it was Kelly-Ann.

The darkness was total. Not a glimmer of light entered the house. It felt suffocating and eerie. Prickles of fear ran down Tom's body, making the hairs on his arms and legs stand on end. What if the elephants had come back? What if they were out there, just outside the house, about to attack it?

Then, from far way, he heard someone call out, and another voice answer with a laugh. The farmers were still out there then, in the fields, keeping the elephants away. He tried to visualize them, down there by their campfires, but all he could see was Kawira on the ground, her slim little body hunched over her baby brother, hopelessly trying to protect him from a maddened elephant.

I couldn't have done that, he thought.

He remembered Mum, and his anxiety returned. Mum might not be faced with a rampaging elephant every night, but she was still in danger. Something could go wrong with her or the baby.

He hadn't given the baby much thought up till now. It had seemed like a nuisance more than anything else, taking his room and making Mum tired and irritable. He tried to imagine what it would be like, a real baby, smaller than Eliud of course, but just as sweet, just as dependent.

He doesn't have to be like Bella, he thought. He'll probably be really great.

He thought of what it would feel like, looking after the baby the way Kawira looked after Eliud. He liked the idea.

He yawned. There must still be hours to go before morning. He'd have to get back to sleep again. He turned over, trying not to wake Joseph who was breathing quietly and regularly on the mat beside him, fast asleep.

He shut his eyes. At once he saw, in his mind's eye, the great bulk of the elephant again, running after him, its trunk raised, its fearsome scream splitting his ears.

Then something occurred to him and he opened his eyes and stared into the dark. The elephant could easily have caught up with him and trampled him to death. He could have killed Kawira and Eliud too, and the farmer who had jumped away down the bank. But each time, at the last moment, he had stopped and veered away. In the end, the only thing he had destroyed, in an awesome display of strength and anger, had been that tree. It was as if his charges had been mock charges, as if his intention had been to frighten, not to kill.

He scared the hell out of me all right, anyway, thought Tom. He was kind of wonderful too, though. I'll never forget him as long as I live.

He moved around on the hard ground, trying to get into a comfortable position without disturbing Joseph.

Think of something nice, he told himself. Nice and quiet and peaceful, that will make me go to sleep.

It was funny, but Kawira came into his mind again, standing by the door with the light behind her, holding Eliud up to someone. Then the picture faded, and he was asleep.

The sound of creaking hinges woke him up as Titus opened the door on to the outside world. Light flooded into the house and Tom, sitting up with a jerk, had to put his hand over his eyes to shield them from the brightness.

He looked round. Joseph was leaning up on one elbow, yawning and rubbing his eyes. Kelly-Ann and Kawira were stirring, in a confusion of arms and legs and blankets.

Tom stood up and staggered sleepily to the door. The crisp fresh air hit him like the invigorating blast of a cold shower but the sun, which had just risen above the shoulder of the mountain, was already deliciously warm. Tom stretched, shook himself and looked round.

The village below was waking up. Women were setting off with their empty jerrycans to fetch water from the stand pipe and coils of pale smoke were rising from the breakfast fires. A group of men sat wearily together under a tree, talking. Tom guessed they had been up all night, guarding their fields.

Just outside the village the sun sparkled on the glass and metal of the jeep, which stood by the side of the track. Daniel was squatting beside it, rinsing out his mouth from a bottle of water.

Above everything floated the peaks of Mount Kenya, wreathed with a coronet of mist, which lay, too, in patches on the ruff of dark green forest. The sky was a perfect translucent blue.

Tom breathed in, filling his lungs with air that was so fresh and pure it tasted like nectar on his tongue. Sounds travelled from far away, as clear as bells – the bark of a dog, the ring of an axe, a child's cries, the bray of a donkey, the clattering alarm call of the troop of Syke's monkeys, who were bounding across an open stretch of ground between their favourite trees, their tails streaming out behind them.

'Oo, I didn't sleep a wink all night. I'm all covered in bruises,' said Kelly-Ann, who had come out of the house and was standing beside Tom, blinking in the strong morning light. She looked up at Titus. 'Have those horrible elephants really gone away?'

'Horrible?' Tom raised his eyebrows. 'I thought you loved elephants.'

Kelly-Ann shuddered.

'Do me a favour! Not after last night I don't. I never want to see an elephant again for the rest of my life.'

Titus looked quizzically at her.

'No more elephants? Eh, that's sad. You've only seen them being frightening, warning the people that they can be dangerous when they can't have what they want. You've never seen elephants as they really are, how they live together in their families.'

'Where are they now, Uncle Titus?' asked Tom. 'Do you think they've gone far away?'

'I don't know. You'll have to ask Daniel. He studies their movements every day. If anyone knows where they are, it's Daniel.'

Daniel had seen Titus up on the hillside and he was running swiftly up the path towards them.

He stopped, slightly out of breath, and saluted smartly.

'*Jambo, bwana. Habari?*' he said.

'*Mzuri sana,*' said Titus.

'Where are all the elephants now, Daniel?' asked Tom. 'Will they . . .' he coughed to steady his voice, 'will they come back this morning?'

Daniel shook his head.

'No. They are waking up quietly in the forest. Maybe soon they will go for their bath, when the sun is a little higher.'

'Their bath?' An image of an enormous bathtub and gigantic taps and towels the size of a tennis court flitted through Tom's mind, and he chuckled.

Kelly-Ann looked anxiously at Daniel.

'There's no water or anything, though, is there, round here? I bet they're miles away.'

'It's not so far.' Daniel pointed to a low ridge on the far side of the village. 'There's a stream over there and a pool. I watch them there very often. There's a good place on the ridge, high up, where it's safe and easy to observe them.'

Tom felt his throat constrict nervously, but all the same he said, 'Are you going there this morning? Can I go with you?'

Daniel looked up at Titus, who nodded.

'Yes, if you like.' His face broke into a smile. 'You're not scared?'

'No,' said Tom untruthfully.

He did feel scared. In fact, his knees felt weak at the thought of being close to elephants again, and yet he wanted more than anything else to watch them properly, to see them without being seen.

'I'm not going,' said Kelly-Ann. 'Catch me going near elephants again.'

Tom felt irrationally annoyed.

'If Daniel says it's safe, it's safe,' he snapped. 'I'm going anyway, and so's Joseph, aren't you?' He looked at Joseph who nodded, then at Titus. 'So that leaves you here on your own.'

Kelly-Ann bit her lip. Titus patted her shoulder.

'Don't be afraid,' he said. 'We'll be on the top of a cliff. The elephants will be below us.'

'You said we'd be safe when we came up here,' said Kelly-Ann rudely, 'and look what happened.'

Titus shook his head.

'She's a tough one, this Kelly-Ann,' he said to Tom. 'What are we going to do with her?'

'Leave her behind,' said Tom, exasperated.

'No, it's OK, I'll come,' Kelly-Ann said hastily.

'Breakfast is ready!' called out Mrs Echessa from the doorway behind them. 'I have cooked some eggs for you.'

'I don't like . . .' began Kelly-Ann. She caught Tom's eye and stopped. 'OK, OK. I'm coming.'

The jeep was crammed with people when they set off after breakfast to see the elephants. Mr Echessa sat in front with Titus, while Daniel squashed in with Tom, Joseph, Kawira and Kelly-Ann in the back.

The world, bathed in early dew, looked freshly washed and new. Brilliant green and gold roller birds swooped low over the grass, their shining feathers dazzling in the sunlight. A cloud of brightly coloured butterflies hovered over a flowering bush. Once, Joseph clutched Tom's arm to point out a porcupine scurrying across a field, its bristles lowered.

Titus parked the jeep at the foot of a sharp wooded rise, and everyone except Mr Echessa got out.

'Are you coming with us?' Titus asked him.

Mr Echessa shook his head.

'I have seen too many elephants,' he said. 'I shall wait here in the car for you.'

'Where's my sunblock?' said Kelly-Ann. 'Hold on, everyone. I've got to get it out of my bag.'

She reached into the back of the jeep and began to unzip her bag. She fished out her tube of sun-block and unscrewed the lid. Titus took the tube out of her hand, screwed the lid back on and tucked it firmly back into her bag.

'Put on your hat and pull down your sleeves to cover your arms,' he said. 'Elephants can pick up a scent like this from two miles away. They might have smelled it already.'

'It depends which way the wind is blowing though, doesn't it?' said Tom.

He didn't want to admit it, but he was feeling scared about being close to elephants again.

'Yes.' Titus nodded towards Daniel. 'Have you got the ashes?'

'Yes, sir.'

Daniel held up a bulging square of cloth tied in a knot.

'Ashes? What for? What do you want ashes for?' demanded Kelly-Ann.

'You'll see,' said Titus, setting off up the path.

It was a short sharp climb. When they were nearly at the top, Titus stopped and everyone came to a halt behind him. He put his finger to his lips.

'From now on, we must talk only quietly if we wish to observe the elephants as they really are. Now, let's test for wind direction. Daniel?'

Daniel untied the knot in the square of cloth, scrambled up on to a boulder, and threw the ashes it contained high up into the air. They floated slowly away, back towards the jeep.

'Good!' whispered Joseph, his face breaking into a smile of understanding. 'The wind's blowing away from us. They won't smell us so easily, will they?'

'No.' Titus was moving cautiously towards the crest of the ridge. 'But we must still be quiet.'

Tom's pulse quickened nervously as he scrambled up the last few metres. He reached the top and looked over the edge, down the steep wooded drop on the other side.

Below him was a deep pool fringed with trees, and on the far side a herd of elephants was standing at the water's edge.

They looked calm and relaxed, their bodies rolling from side to side as they moved around the pool, their great feet padding softly on the dusty ground. Their trunks swung gently with the rhythm of their steps and their ears flapped a little, not with the terrifying clapping stiffness of aggression, but as if they simply wanted to fan themselves.

Tom dug Joseph in the ribs.

'I've just noticed something,' he whispered. 'Their ears are the same shape as Africa.'

The elephants were approaching each other, lifting their trunks and gently touching each other's faces.

'It's their way of greeting,' said Daniel softly. 'Can you see how that one is putting the tip of her trunk into the other one's mouth? It's like shaking hands for them.'

'But why do they need to greet each other?' whispered Tom. 'They're together all the time, aren't they?'

'Not all the time.' Daniel's eyes were narrowed against the light as he counted the elephants and noted down the number on the pad he was carrying. 'There are two families here. Can you see the biggest one with the long curved tusks? She's the grandmother, the matriarch. She's nearly sixty years old. And that other big one, she's her younger sister. They bring their families together here usually to bathe, then they go off to feed separately.'

'They don't wash properly though, do they?' said Kelly-Ann, whose confidence was growing again now that the elephants were at a safe distance. 'I mean they're all covered with dried mud.'

'They like that,' said Titus. 'They're like women with their face packs. The mud is good for their skin. They plaster it on themselves and throw dust all over it, then they rub themselves against a tree or a rock and all the little ticks and parasites come off with the mud.'

'Ticks? Parasites?' squeaked Kelly-Ann too loudly.

Tom was about to dig her in the ribs and tell her to be quiet when Joseph hissed excitedly, 'Look! They're going into the water!'

Titus shook his head at them both, putting his finger on his lips again.

The first elephant, the big grandmother, had reached the water's edge. She dropped her trunk into it and swished it around for a moment, churning up the leaves of the water plants that were floating on the surface. Then, with a low growl of pleasure, she waded deep into the pool and sank down into the water, completely disappearing except for her trunk, which, black with muddy wetness, waved above the surface like a gigantic periscope.

One by one the others followed her. They dived and wallowed, rolled and splashed, sucking up water with their trunks and squirting it out again, lovingly nudging and caressing each other, slapping their wet ears against their heads.

Tom watched them, entranced. They were gentle, happy, relaxed, at ease with themselves. It was better than anything he could have imagined. He'd never seen anything like it. 'They're playing!' he breathed.

'Yes. They're just having fun.' Titus spoke quietly but above a whisper, knowing that the noise the elephants were making would cover his voice.

A little elephant calf, no more than a metre tall, hovered uncertainly on the edge of the pool, not daring to move in further than the shallow strip of water at the edge. She took a few steps into the water, missed her footing, and fell with a splash. She squealed indignantly and at once an older elephant, hovering nearby, pushed her upright with her leg, then sucked up a trunkful of water and squirted it all over her. It excited the baby and she began to run about at the edge of the pool, scattering a flock of wading birds and charging with babyish fervour at a floating log.

Another elephant suddenly emerged from the

trees at the edge of the clearing and stood watching for a moment before he ran into the water to join them. Titus raised the binoculars which he was carrying on a strap round his neck.

'It's the young bull who chased you yesterday,' he said gently. 'Look, you can see the wound on his face, beneath his ear.'

The young elephant, eager to get into the water, ran into the pool too hastily and knocked against a small female, hitting her with his strong muscular trunk. One of the biggest elephants, who had been slumped blissfully up to her shoulders in mud, rose with a sudden roar and faced him, her ears out at full stretch. The young male tossed his head up and down for a moment or two, then turned round and, his short tufted tail swinging, disappeared up the path.

'What's the matter?' Joseph said, turning to Titus. 'Why are they chasing him away?'

'They're all females and calves here,' answered Titus. 'He's getting too old now to stay with them. He's probably annoying them, being too aggressive and rough all the time. He has to grow up and go out into the world. He'll join with some other males and they'll live together. It's probably his own mother who is sending him away.'

'That's awful,' whispered Tom. 'That's so sad. He's been driven out of his own family.'

'He'll be fine,' said Titus, 'when his wound has healed. He'll make friends and live with them. It's only hard for him now, for a few months, while he's learning to be independent. Even human beings have to do that.'

'Is that why he attacked us yesterday, because he was kind of upset?' asked Tom. 'And he's got that wound on top of everything else.'

'Maybe. I don't know.'

The elephants had finished their bath. One by one, with leisurely rumblings, they were ambling out of the water.

Tom watched them thoughtfully.

'They're sort of like us, like human beings,' he said. 'Except that they're different too. I mean, they're in a family. They like being with their family.' Something was tickling him. He looked down and saw a huge ant racing up his leg. He flicked it off. 'And they even have rows some-times, too.'

10

A GOOD IDEA

No one stirred for a moment or two after the last elephants had gone, swaying silently away among the trees, their little tails swinging like short thin ropes between their ponderous thighs.

Daniel moved first. He pulled out a pad and ballpoint pen and started making notes.

Joseph looked curiously over his arm.

'I have to monitor the elephants' daily movements,' said Daniel, looking up at him.

'Where are they going now?' asked Kawira anxiously.

'They are moving in a westerly direction,' said Daniel, wrinkling his nose as he looked up towards the sun. 'They're going off to feed, looking for good grass and any trees with their favourite fruits on them. Eh, listen. You can even hear them now. I do not think they will return to the village today.'

They all cocked their heads and listened. Loud trumpetings and rumblings could be heard from inside the forest, moving gradually away.

'Did you see the baby?' said Kelly-Ann. 'Did

you see him sort of sneeze when he got mud stuck in his trunk?'

Tom took off and began to run down the track. He didn't want to talk about the elephants. He wanted to keep the sight and sound of them quietly in his head like a secret.

He speeded up, jumping recklessly over the steep bits. He sensed Joseph, lured into a race, hard on his heels. They tore neck and neck across the last flat stretch to the jeep and collapsed beside it.

'You know about that elephant god in India?' panted Joseph. 'I'd believe in him if I was them.'

'Yes,' said Tom shortly. He didn't even want to discuss the elephants with Joseph.

From further up the track they could hear Kelly-Ann complaining loudly to Titus about a stone in her sandal.

'I don't get it,' said Tom. 'Why doesn't Titus belt her one? She's so rude to him and he just takes it. He'd kill you if you spoke to him like that. Or if I did. Except that we wouldn't, either of us.'

'Kill us? No, he would just look at us from up above, like some big giraffe who is going to tread on a worm. That would be much worse.'

'Yeah, you're right.'

'He's sorry for her, I think. He told me she reminds him of Lucky.'

'Who's Lucky?'

'A chimp. Uncle Titus rescued her from smug-glers when she was little and sort of brought her up. Lucky was kind of sad. Uncle Titus said sometimes she used to like biting people, and then she tried to cuddle them, but too much.'

Tom sighed.

'Yeah, that's Kelly-Ann. She'd be easier to live with though, wouldn't she, if she really was a chimp.'

The others reached them. Kelly-Ann and Kawira climbed into the jeep. Mr Echessa hadn't said a word all morning but now he and Titus began to talk in Swahili, Mr Echessa spreading out his hands and gesticulating as if he was trying to convince Titus of something. Tom could hear the English words 'electric fence' repeated several times.

At last Titus turned round.

'Listen, kids,' he said. 'I have to go back to the village and talk to everyone there again. I was going to take you to Meru this morning but . . .'

'Oh, we don't mind,' said Tom.

Joseph nodded matter-of-factly, and Kawira looked confused. She wasn't used to being con-sulted.

They all turned to look uneasily at Kelly-Ann. She tossed her head.

'I don't mind,' she said. 'I like it here. Me and Kawira are going to look for those monkeys again, aren't we, Kawira?'

The drive back to the village seemed much shorter. Titus pulled up in his old parking place. A crowd of villagers was waiting for them. They parted silently as Titus and Mr Echessa walked through them, then followed them into the open space in the middle of the village.

The four children sat down in the shade of a nearby tree.

'What do you think, then? Will Titus agree about trying to get an electric fence?' said Tom.

Joseph shrugged.

'How could I know? You heard what he said.'

'It could work though, couldn't it?' said Tom.

'We want them at least to try it,' said Kawira. 'We cannot continue living in this way.'

'Wish we could think of a better way out of all this.' Tom picked up a stick and began drawing in the dust with it. 'I mean, the elephants think this is their place and the people do too. You can't exactly go up to the elephants and say, "Look here guys, we'll give you this field if you'll leave that one alone." '

'What are you on about?' demanded Kelly-Ann.

'I mean they both want the crops.' Tom was frowning, following his train of thought. 'But if they wanted different things—'

'That baby elephant,' interrupted Kelly-Ann, who was getting bored. 'It was so cute. I mean its darling little legs, and its weeny trunk, and the way it mucked about, just like a sweet little puppy or something. I wish my mum could have seen it.'

Tom nodded.

'I wish Afra could have seen them and all. She'd have gone crazy.'

'My father used to take tourists to see the elephants,' Kawira said. 'He used to drive them up to a special place to watch them.'

'Tourists would pay a fortune to watch them like we did today,' said Tom. 'I mean up there above the pool – that was a brilliant place.'

Suddenly he sat bolt upright, his eyes shining.

'That's it!' he said. 'That's the answer! Bring tourists here! Set up a base for them. The farmers could show them round and everything, and get paid for it. They wouldn't have to go on being farmers so they wouldn't have to fight the elephants.'

'It would not be possible,' said Kawira. 'Tourists like too much to have big hotels, with bathrooms and many luxurious things. My father used to tell me. Bars, restaurants, expensive food – we do not have anything like that here. Everyone here is very much poor.'

Tom subsided, discouraged. Nobody spoke for a moment.

'Tom's right.' Joseph had been sitting with his arms wrapped around his knees but now he straightened up and began waving his hands excitedly in the air. 'It's a very fine idea. They could build a beautiful hotel here. It's a great place. Look at it!' He waved his arms, nearly hitting Tom on the nose. 'The forest is so close by. It must be full of animals.'

He put his head back and whooped like a hyena.

'Are you kidding?' said Kelly-Ann. 'There isn't even any electricity here.'

'We had electricity before,' said Kawira. 'It became broken down. They never fixed it.'

'Then they can bring it back!' Tom stood up, fired by his dream.

Joseph squinted up at him against the light.

'But it would cost too much money to build a proper hotel here. Millions and millions of shillings. Where would you get the money?'

Tom said nothing. He was thinking furiously.

'Afra told me about a place she went to once, with the wildlife club at school,' he said at last. 'It wasn't posh at all. It had lots of tents and a kind of central building – a nice old house – where the teachers stayed, and a dining room place and showers and stuff like that. Loads of people go there all the time. Campers and backpackers and people. There could be a place like that here, you know, that wouldn't cost a bomb to stay at.'

Joseph still wasn't convinced.

'Even to buy the land and build a house you

would need too much money,' he said depressively.

'Oh!' Kawira suddenly jumped to her feet. 'We would not need to build a house, only to repair one. There is an old place near here, a *mzungu*'s* house, that has been empty for many years.'

'A house wouldn't be big enough,' objected Kelly-Ann. 'You can't make hotels just out of houses.'

'But it is a big house, very big,' said Kawira. 'The *mzungu* died there ten, fifteen years ago.' She dropped her voice. 'He was killed by others. No one dares to go near there now.'

'You mean he was murdered? It's haunted?' said Tom.

'Haunted?' Kelly-Ann gave a little scream. 'I'm not going there. Catch me going anywhere haunted.'

'I'm not scared,' said Tom. He looked at Joseph. 'What about you?'

Joseph squared his shoulders.

'Has anyone seen this spirit?' he asked Kawira.

'No. They are just afraid. They fear that the *mzungu*'s spirit might be very angry. That is why they leave the place alone.'

'Well, I vote we go and have a look at it,' said Tom. 'I mean, if it turns out it's a nice house and it could be done up into a hotel, it would be so

* white person's

106

brilliant. There would be loads of jobs for everyone. Even the ghost. He'd make a brilliant night watchman.'

'My mother would be the cook,' said Kawira, her eyes shining.

'And those men who lit all the fires last night, they would be the guards,' said Joseph.

'And we'd come and organize football matches for the campers,' said Tom, dribbling an imaginary ball in a circle round the others.

'And I would have a lovely little shop and sell all elephant things in it,' said Kelly-Ann.

They stopped and looked at each other.

'Come on,' said Tom. 'What are we waiting for? Let's go and look at the house. Show us the way, Kawira!'

11

THE DEAD MZUNGU

Kawira shook her head regretfully.

'I would like to come with you,' she said, 'but my mother will not allow me. I have to take care of Eliud, and there are many other things I must do for her.'

There was a disappointed silence. Everyone had been getting excited about looking for the old house.

'Wait a minute,' said Tom. 'Couldn't we take Eliud with us? And we could give you a hand if there's anything your mum wants you to do before you go.'

Kawira giggled.

'You cannot fetch the water or sweep the floor,' she said. 'You are boys.'

'Who says?' Tom banged himself on the chest, pleased to have made Kawira laugh. 'Try us.'

They followed Kawira back to her house. Grace was trying to hold Eliud back from crawling into the ashes of the fire. His round cheeks creased into a smile of delight when he saw Kawira and he waved his hands, already grey with ashes, in a dancing welcome. Grace greeted Kawira with a frown and a stream of Swahili, but when Kawira replied she chuckled and pointed to two empty jerrycans by the door.

'Take them!' she said to the boys. 'Do not spill the water when you return!'

Tom and Joseph picked up the jerrycans and dashed off to the stand pipe.

'They'd have to have lots of running water if they built a hotel,' said Tom. 'Tourists all want showers and toilets and stuff.'

Joseph turned on the tap. Water gushed out of it.

'There's plenty here,' he said, holding his can under the flow. 'Try a little.'

He squirted some at Tom. Tom ducked too late, and water splashed on his face and hair.

'Right!' he said joyfully. 'I'll get you for that!'

He was about to splosh some water over Joseph when whoops and cackles came from behind them. A crowd of girls and women were pointing at them, rocking backwards and forwards with laughter. Tom laughed too, filling his jerrycan to the brim, but Joseph looked embarrassed.

'They're saying we are girls,' he said disgustedly. 'This is a woman's job.'

They got back to Grace's little house. Kawira was sweeping out the floor while Kelly-Ann sat outside with Eliud on her knee. Susanna, her shyness gone, was dancing in front of Kelly-Ann, making her laugh.

Grace came out of the house, grinning broadly at Tom and Joseph.

'Oh, what lovely brides you will be for some lucky husbands,' she said.

'Thank you,' said Tom in a high squeaky voice. He reverted to his normal one. 'Can Kawira come with us now please?'

'Yes, she can go,' said Grace, taking Eliud off Kelly-Ann's lap and spilling a little of the precious water onto the ground as she washed his hands and face. She transferred him to Kawira's arms. 'Be careful with him now. Do not drop him in front of any elephants again.'

They set off at once, before Grace could change her mind, back down the track they'd come up in the jeep the day before. A few hundred metres below the village, Kawira struck off on a path to the left, and they followed her in single file between fields of newly sprouting maize. Bright orange flowers that smelled of guavas bloomed in the low hedges on either side, and once or twice Tom saw a tiny jewel-like bird hopping from twig to twig.

The path had joined an old track now. It was well-trodden at first, but as they went on, climbing a little, it became rougher and more overgrown. Old ruts showed that cars had used it once, but seasons of heavy rain and the thick growth of many years had long since made it impassable. No car would be able to get up it now.

The track turned a sudden corner and all four of them stopped and gasped.

Ahead was an old house, long and low, its walls made of grey stone, its roof of corrugated iron sheets. Rickety wooden steps led up to a verandah which must have been beautiful once, though its faded green paint was peeling now. On either side of it was a big bay window, almost covered with a wild profusion of pink roses which reached up over the house, half smothering one corner.

'There's loads of room for tents here,' said Tom. 'This must have been a garden once.'

'There was a very beautiful garden,' nodded Kawira. 'My grandmother told me. The old *mzungu* woman used to grow many flowers. Slowly by slowly, it has grown over.'

Joseph was looking back along the track.

'The road's very bad,' he said. 'You can't even drive a tractor up here.' He walked a little way round the side of the house. 'Eh, this would be a good place for a car park – under this old tree.'

'You'd have to get rid of all these bushes and stuff,' said Kelly-Ann. 'It's a real old jungle. Hey! What's that?'

She grabbed Kawira's arm, startling Eliud, who was tied in a cloth to Kawira's back and had been asleep, his head lolling against her shoulder.

'It's only a rock hyrax,' said Tom, watching a little brown creature the size of a big rabbit, bolting under the protective shadow of a bush.

Its round whiskered face watched them for a moment or two, nose twitching, before it disappeared.

'I thought for a moment it was a rat,' said Kelly-Ann, puckering up her mouth. 'I just go crazy if I see a rat, even on TV.'

Tom wasn't listening to her. He was assessing the house with narrowed eyes.

'The rooms look big enough,' he said. 'You could probably have bars and restaurants and things in them.' He turned to Kawira. 'How far back does it go? How many other rooms are there?'

'I do not know,' said Kawira, jiggling Eliud up and down to soothe him. 'But it is big. I think there are many rooms.'

'You don't have to have only tents,' said Kelly-Ann, following Tom's train of thought. 'You could have chalets too, all round the main bit. Me and Mum stayed in a hotel with chalets once. It was brilliant.'

Joseph had started pushing his way through the undergrowth at the side of the house, trying to get round to the back.

'You can come this way!' he called to the others. 'There's a little path here.'

The path had clearly been made by animals, and the children had to bend down under the low bushes that closed over their heads.

'I don't like this,' said Kelly-Ann. 'It might have been leopards or something that made this path.'

'Very strange leopards,' said Joseph, pointing to a hard little mound of dung. 'They make the droppings of bushbuck.'

They emerged suddenly on to a flat rock, and stood upright.

'Wow! Amazing!' gasped Tom. 'I don't believe it!'

The land fell away from beneath their feet into a spectacular vista of trees and fields, rolling down to a golden plain, on the far side of which a range of hills shimmered in a purple heat haze.

'I mean, it's just incredible! Like you're in an aeroplane or something.' He turned to Joseph.

Joseph nodded, unimpressed. He was used to the stunning views of his country and took them for granted.

'Tourists will like this, won't they?' he said, batting a fly off his ear.

'Like it? They'll love it!'

Tom looked at the house. Kawira was right. It was big. Another verandah, even more elaborately carved than the one at the front, ran the entire length of the back rooms. An old table and two old armchairs, whose rusty springs were protruding from their seats, still stood on it.

There was a sudden crashing noise in the trees that covered the steep slope below them, and the leaves shook violently.

'Monkeys,' said Kawira nonchalantly, hitching Eliud into a more comfortable position. 'Colobus monkeys. Eh, eh, there are too many of them.'

A monkey chose that moment to make a spectacular flying leap from one branch to another, its long black arms reaching out like slender grappling hooks. Tom screwed up his eyes to see better, and caught the flash of white hair that fringed the monkey's slim black back.

'It's too far!' squealed Kelly-Ann. 'He'll fall!'

'They never fall,' said Tom, but he held his breath all the same.

The monkey landed, grabbing hold of a thin branch which plunged violently down with his weight, then shot up again, took another expert leap and disappeared into the tree's thick foliage.

'The guests could all sit out on the verandah and watch them,' said Joseph.

'And they could have those stripy umbrellas over the tables, and loads of nice drinks,' said Kelly-Ann.

They turned round and studied the back of the house.

'The door's open! Look!' said Joseph.

Tom looked. Joseph was right. The door leading into the house from the verandah was swinging open on its hinges.

'Come on,' he said. 'Let's go inside.'

No one moved.

'You're not scared, are you?' said Tom, looking at their blank faces. 'No one's here now.'

'He was murdered,' said Kawira. 'The *mzungu* was murdered.'

Tom stopped. The vacant windows of the house suddenly looked like dead eyes. He felt his flesh creep.

'What happened?' he said to Kawira.

She looked at him, her eyes wide and serious.

'They found him here. He was lying on his bed. Someone had cut him like this' – she drew a line from her neck to her waist – 'with a knife. His blood had splashed everywhere, on the walls and the floor.'

'Why?' said Joseph. 'Who would do such a thing?'

Kawira dropped her voice, as if she was almost afraid the dead man would hear her, and the others crowded round to listen, jostling Eliud, who gave a snuffling snort in his sleep.

'He was a madman,' she said. 'The father, the old *mzungu*, he came here first. He cut down the forest where we have our farms now. He was not so bad. He planted big fields of wheat. Many white men came from England to visit him and shoot elephants. But then he died and his son was here alone. He used to drink too much beer. He beat his servants and the farmworkers. He was like a . . . a . . .'

'A tyrant,' said Tom.

'Yes, a tyrant. When he was drinking, he was so angry! He did not like anyone to come close to the house.

'There was a woman, her house was very close to here, and she and her family always walked this way to fetch their water. There was no other way for them to go. One day, this mad *mzungu*, he saw her walking past his house. He took his gun and he shot at her. He hit the baby that she was carrying on her back. The baby died.'

She lifted the cloth that tied Eliud to her back to ease the weight on her shoulders.

'After a week, they found the *mzungu* like I told you, on his bed, dead. There was a cut in him, right down his whole body.'

'He deserved it,' said Tom, startling himself and the others by speaking loudly. He looked defiantly up at the house. 'I'm not scared. I'm going in.'

'He's not still in there, is he?' said Kelly-Ann, shivering.

'Of course he is not there,' said Kawira. 'A lot of *mzungu* people came and buried him in the churchyard in Meru.'

'Anyway, I'm not going in,' said Kelly-Ann. 'You never know what you might be getting into, in a place like this.'

Tom and Joseph exchanged looks.

'I'll come,' said Joseph, frowning nervously.

'Good,' said Tom, secretly relieved. He hadn't liked the idea of going into the house on his own.

The two boys began to push their way through the thick bushes towards the verandah steps. Kawira followed them.

Tom turned round.

'Are you coming too, then?' he said to her.

She smiled at him.

'I do not want to go in there alone,' she said, 'but if I am with you I will feel safe.'

Tom felt his cheeks burn with pleasure. He turned again to follow Joseph, who was almost at the verandah steps.

'Hey, don't leave me here on my own!' Kelly-Ann called after them. 'Don't go without me! Wait!'

The others didn't stop.

'Oh, all right,' she said crossly. 'I'll come. But if we get murdered ourselves, don't blame me, that's all.'

12

THE DESERTED HOUSE

The wooden steps leading up to the house were frayed and soggy with rot and everyone had to be careful where they put their feet, but the floor of the verandah, protected as it was by the corrugated iron roof, was solid. Dead leaves and bird droppings were strewn everywhere and it was obvious that no one had been here for a long time.

The door was ajar. Tom hesitated for a moment, his ears keenly tuned to any sound from inside, his skin prickling with anticipation. Then he felt a nudge from Joseph and gave the door a push. It resisted. He pushed a little harder. It gave way suddenly and swung open, the groan of its rusting hinges making Kawira squeak with fright.

Gingerly Tom stepped inside. A corridor ran ahead of him. The pattern on the old strip of carpet was almost invisible under the accumulation of grime and drifting leaves, but the cream paint on the walls still looked surprisingly fresh, and an unbroken lampshade hung from the ceiling.

Doors led off to the left and right. The first was

shut. Tom hesitated for a moment, his hand on the doorknob, but a horrid picture came into his mind of the dead *mzungu*, his torso slashed from neck to groin, lying with staring eyes on a blood-soaked bed. He felt his hair stand on end and went on.

The next door was open, and the four children crowded round to look inside. It had once been a bedroom. The bed frame was still there, though the mattress had gone, and an old-fashioned washstand stood between the two windows, a blue china jug and basin still on it. Faded chintz curtains, stained with damp and thin with age, fluttered gently in the breeze that blew in through a broken window pane.

'Eh, man, what if it happened in here?' whispered Joseph.

'Do not say it! You will frighten me too much,' Kawira whispered back.

Tom was already moving on down the corridor, glancing up at the pictures of English bluebell woods and Cornish coves that still hung on the walls.

The corridor opened out on to a wide vestibule, with the front door and verandah at the far end. The sun was shining brightly in through the dirty windows. It was easy to imagine people living here, children running in and out from the garden, adults talking and laughing as they walked up the steps to the front door.

Tom stopped and the others, who had been following close behind, almost bumped into him.

'It's like someone really old still lives here,' he said in a normal voice. 'It smells like my great-gran's house did.'

They'd been sticking close together, but now felt bold enough to move apart. Joseph went over to the light switch beside the front door and tried flicking it on and off. Nothing happened. Kelly-Ann sat down on an old sofa under the window. Puffs of dust rose up from it and she jumped up again, coughing. Kawira stood looking curiously at a picture of an English cottage with a thatched roof and a garden full of hollyhocks.

'You know in hotels,' said Tom, 'there's always a kind of desk and the keys are all hung up behind it and there's someone who tells you where your bedroom is?'

Kawira and Joseph looked mystified.

'You mean Reception,' said Kelly-Ann scornfully. 'That's what it's called.'

'Well, this is the place for it, right here,' said Tom, going over to stand in the corner opposite the door.

He'd never stayed in a hotel but he'd seen them often on TV. He could picture it all – the cars pulling up and boys in uniforms running out to bring in the luggage, and the manager surging towards them with his hands held out, beaming a welcome. He tried to imagine Mr Echessa inside the manager's suit. It was easy.

'It'd be amazing,' he said. 'It would be a brilliant hotel.'

Three doors led off the vestibule. Kelly-Ann opened the first one and they all looked in. The room was big and sunny, with a huge bay window at one end and a fireplace at the other. There was no furniture in it.

Tom suddenly wanted to look into every room. He tried the door opposite but it was stuck and, too impatient to force it, he ran back up the corridor, the others in his wake, flinging open one door after another. Some rooms were big, others were small, some were empty while in others a few sticks of broken furniture still leaned against the walls or sagged to the floor.

They had forgotten their fear now. They poked into every corner and looked out of every window, writing their names in the grime on the glass. Only Kawira held back. She seemed overwhelmed rather than afraid.

'I have lived very much close to here for so many years,' she said, 'and this is my first time to come inside. I have never seen such a place up till now.'

They congregated at last in the front hall again.

'We haven't gone into this room yet,' said Kelly-Ann, going towards the one remaining closed door.

'I tried it. It's stuck,' said Tom.

Joseph turned the handle, put his shoulder against the door and heaved. It gave suddenly, and he almost fell into the room.

It had clearly been a sitting room once. It was big. There was a fireplace with a mirror, cracked now, above the mantelpiece. Two deep armchairs still sat on either side of the hearth, their upholstery stained and greasy. Below them fine piles of dust showed where insects had been boring into the wood. In one corner was a big cupboard.

The ceiling had given way in one place, and through the hole in it Tom could see daylight. A sheet of corrugated iron in the roof above had come loose and rain had poured in. The floor below, rotten with damp, had disintegrated and pieces of the fallen ceiling had gone right through the floorboards leaving a jagged hole.

'Mind out. That bit of floor looks dodgy,' said Tom to the others, who had followed him into the room.

He felt at ease now, hardly scared at all. He was enjoying himself. He went over to the cupboard and opened it, then jumped back in alarm as a stack of empty whisky bottles cascaded out with a shockingly loud crash.

Kelly-Ann screamed theatrically and clutched at Kawira. Eliud woke up with a snuffly cry. Joseph and Tom, who had both stiffened in fright, giggled with relief and then began to stagger around the room, pretending to be drunk.

'Cheers, me ol' mate,' said Tom, waving a phantom glass in the air.

Joseph pretended to clink it with one of his own, and lurched off into the corner of the room behind one of the armchairs.

'Hic! Oops! Gimme another!'

He stopped dead, swaying slightly forward on his feet and righting himself cautiously.

'What's the matter? What've you fou—'

Joseph's frantic alarm signals silenced Tom. He stood still, watching Joseph, who was cautiously tiptoeing backwards, every muscle tensed.

Tom craned forward, trying to see what Joseph had seen, but a second later he skidded backwards himself as the head of a snake, thick and black, appeared from below the armchair, its tongue flickering. It paused for an eternal moment. Its eye, as bright as glass, seemed to Tom as if it was studying him. Then, as smooth and fast as a stream of oil running over metal, it slid across the floor, length after length of its grey body emerging until it seemed to Tom, frozen in endless time, that it would go on producing more and more of itself for ever.

The tail appeared at last and seconds later the snake had disappeared down a hole in the floor.

'We've got to get out of here! I can't stand this. It'll come back, it'll get us!'

Tom hardly heard Kelly-Ann. He was measuring the distance to the door with his eyes, working out how near they would have to pass to the hole. The snake could easily be lying in wait, just underneath the floorboards, coiled up, ready to strike with lightning precision at their bare legs as they ran past.

His skin was crawling. He had a sudden conviction that there were other snakes in the room, on the floor behind him, about to fall from the ceiling, hiding in the folds of the rotting curtains, lurking in the broken drawers of the old desk in the corner of the room.

He tried to control his shudders and looked round. He couldn't see any more snakes but that didn't mean they weren't there.

'Wait,' he said to Kelly-Ann, who was poised ready to bolt past the hole. 'I'll try the window.'

He tiptoed to the nearest window and pushed down the metal catch. It gave protestingly and he thrust the window open and looked out. There was a tangle of weeds and roses beneath it. They would be scratched to bits by the thorns if they jumped down there, and who knew what other dangers might be lurking underneath? Dozens of puff-adders, hundreds of cobras – he could see their muscular coils now before his eyes.

Compulsively he shut the window and looked desperately around the room. The faded red of an old velvet cushion on one of the armchairs caught his eye and he knew at once what to do. He dashed forward, picked it up and, running over to the hole, dropped it neatly on top, holding it down with trembling hands.

'Go on! Run for it!' he shouted to the others.

They were past him and out of the room in a flash, and a few seconds later they were all in the lane outside the house.

13

DISCUSSION WITH THE ELDERS

They ran full tilt down the lane away from the house, until they had turned the first corner. Eliud, who disliked being bumped around on Kawira's back, set up a protesting cry and Kawira slowed down to a walk. The others followed suit.

'I reckon it was a black mamba,' said Tom, who was walking in the middle of the path, as far as possible from the two dense hedges on either side. He kept eyeing them nervously, afraid of what other horrors they might contain. 'One bite from one of them and you're dead meat. You roll over and swell up, then you can't move, and the next thing you know you've had it.'

Joseph looked doubtful.

'But this snake ran away from us. Mambas, they're very aggressive animals. They'll see you, and say, OK, let's bite him, and then they'll attack. There was a mamba once in my grandfather's village. He crawled down from the roof into the hut of a family and he bit them all in turn. One, two, three – up to seven! In the morning they were all dead.'

'Shut up! Shut up!' cried Kelly-Ann, clapping

her hands over her ears. 'You're giving me the total, total creeps.'

'I do not think it was a mamba.' Kawira was frowning intently. 'I do not think we have seen a snake at all.'

'Of course it was a snake! Didn't you see it?' Kelly-Ann sounded quite indignant.

'I think,' said Kawira in a solemn voice, 'that it was the spirit of the dead *mzungu*.'

Tom felt a shudder start from his chest and spread right down his arms and legs, making all the little hairs on them stand on end.

'No,' he said doubtfully. 'That's daft, that is.'

Kawira tightened her lips and gave her head a tiny shake.

'Such things happen,' said Joseph. 'It can be true. If Kawira's right, the spirit won't be satisfied until the murderers have been punished.'

'But we don't even know who killed him,' said Tom, who had suddenly remembered the bright, knowing eye of the snake and was half convinced.

'We do know,' Kawira nodded. 'It was the husband of the woman he shot. The *mzungu* had also beaten him severely and had killed one of his cows.'

'Where is he now then?' asked Tom.

'The murderer? He is dead,' said Kawira, leading the way out of the overgrown path on to the main track that led to the village. 'He went down to the coast to look for work and he died of malaria.'

'There you are then,' said Tom, secretly relieved. 'If the man who killed him is dead already, the *mzungu*'s spirit doesn't need revenge. Anyway, he got properly buried in the churchyard. You said so.'

'His body, yes, but where is his spirit?' said Kawira simply.

'Tom's right.' Joseph wriggled his shoulders and took a few jogging steps, as if shaking off something that had been weighing him down. 'It was only a snake. I don't believe it was that man's spirit. You said it yourself, Kawira. Nobody goes to that house. Snakes can feel safe there. It's a good place for them.'

'Them? You mean there's more than one?' squealed Kelly-Ann.

'Bound to be,' said Tom. 'Loads of them, I expect.'

Kelly-Ann shook her head.

'My mum's not going to believe this. She asks your mum to have me to sleep over at your house for a couple of nights and I end up in the middle of nowhere, being charged by elephants, sleeping in a hut on the floor, and almost bitten to death by giant poisonous snakes.'

Tom felt his face going red.

'It's not my mum's fault! She can't help being ill. She was doing your mum a favour, and it's not as if she didn't have enough to do anyway, with the baby coming so soon and all.'

They had nearly reached the village. Joseph frowned disapprovingly at Kelly-Ann.

'You were not nearly bitten by the snake,' he said. 'He took one look at you and ran away. Also, you don't know if he was poisonous.'

Kelly-Ann shuddered.

'Oh, he was poisonous all right. I could tell.'

They had arrived back at Mr Echessa's compound. The area outside his door was crowded with the men of the village, standing and squatting in a circle around Titus and Mr Echessa who sat side by side on a pair of stools. Titus looked relieved when he saw the four children and waved at them.

'Good! You are here!' he said. 'Daniel looked but he could not find you.'

'Sorry, Titus,' said Tom, feeling a little shy with so many eyes turned on him. 'We had an idea. We wanted to see if it could work out.'

'Tell me about it later,' said Titus, signalling to the four of them to sit down at the edge of the crowd. He turned back to Mr Echessa and began to talk to him earnestly again in Swahili. But Mr Echessa, who seemed to want a diversion, beckoned Tom forward.

'Come,' he said. 'Tell us what you have been thinking. Out of the mouths of babes and sucklings, eh, Mr Musau? If you will not give us our electric fence, we must think of another way to protect ourselves from the elephants. Perhaps this young man will help us.'

Blushing hotly, Tom went through to the middle of the circle, dragging a reluctant Joseph behind him. Kawira, overcome with shyness in the presence of the village elders, had slipped round the corner of the house. Kelly-Ann had sat down on a log and taken off her shoe, shaking it out to get rid of a stone.

'Well,' said Tom. 'We were wondering, I mean we thought, because you and the elephants both want the same things, I mean the crops, and it's so difficult to make them go away, but people like seeing elephants. Tourists do, anyway, so if they came here they'd pay for it, and there would be jobs for everyone running things for them and you wouldn't have to go on being farmers.'

He stopped, embarrassed, afraid he'd made a fool of himself.

Mr Echessa threw back his head and laughed, slapping his thigh with the flat of his broad hand.

'Eh, eh! This is a very intelligent boy. Very good, Tom! We also have had the same idea, to make a lodge here for tourists. Many, many times we have discussed it among ourselves.'

The circle of men around him nodded.

'Oh,' said Tom, crestfallen. 'But don't you think it's possible?'

'Tourists like to have many things, a hotel, good

roads, electricity. This costs so much money. Where is the money for such a project?'

'We thought about that,' said Tom eagerly. 'That's where we've been. I mean, Kawira told us about the old *mzungu*'s house and we reckoned it might be a good place for a hotel. We were thinking, it wouldn't have to be a really expensive hotel, more kind of like a camping place with a hotel bit in the middle with a restaurant and things. And the *mzungu*'s house is massive. You'd only have to repair it. Everything's there.'

Mr Echessa leaned forward, pulled Tom towards himself and patted him on the back. He was still chuckling.

'Tom, Tom, you will be a great man one day. A politician! This *mzungu*'s house, too, we have considered it many times. But the ownership is not in our hands. It is the property now of a businessman in Nairobi. We do not have access to this person. We do not know how to approach him.'

'Oh, sorry. We just thought . . . I mean it seemed like a good idea.'

'It *is* a good idea. It's a very good idea.' Titus, who had been leaning forward on his stool, his elbows on his knees, sat up. 'Well done, you guys.'

'It was all of us really,' mumbled Tom. 'Kawira showed us the house. And Kelly-Ann was there too,' he added conscientiously.

'Tom, you've come up with something

important,' Titus went on. 'It's certainly something for us to consider.' He turned to Mr Echessa. 'Why didn't you suggest it before?'

Mr Echessa shook his head ruefully.

'All of us have discussed these matters many times. We decided that an electric fence is best for us.'

'And I have told you, many times,' said Titus, firmly but courteously, 'that electric fences work very well in some places, but they're not the right answer here. The distances are too great. There will be no money for this from KWS.'

'OK, OK. We understand you.' Mr Echessa looked round at the ring of elders, who murmured their assent. 'But to bring tourists here, there are many difficulties. We did not see how it is possible to proceed.'

'We'll have to look into it,' Titus nodded. 'But the kids are right. It doesn't have to be a luxury hotel. It could attract school groups, package tours – yes, I can see it all. Tom, the house is big? In good condition?'

'It's lovely,' said Tom, 'only the roof's fallen in in the sitting room and there's a hole in the floor, and we saw a huge snake in it. A whopper.'

The crowd of people drew in their breath and everyone began talking at once.

'It was a really long snake, three metres at least, and black. I thought it was a mamba. Joseph didn't.'

Titus nodded at his nephew.

'Joseph's right. It couldn't have been a mamba. They're fussy. They only stay in hot places, at low altitude. You'll never find a mamba in this kind of cold place. It was a grass snake perhaps. Probably it wasn't poisonous at all.'

'It was. I know it was,' said Kelly-Ann, who had appeared unexpectedly behind Tom's shoulder. 'Anyway, Kawira thinks it's the spirit of the dead *mzungu*.'

Titus frowned. Mr Echessa, who had been talking to one of the farmers standing beside him, turned back and shook his head seriously.

'It is not,' he said. 'We are not worried now about this old story.' He lifted his baseball cap to scratch his head, then pulled it forward again. 'Many ceremonies have been performed, and there were some among us who witnessed the departure of his spirit. This was a wicked man but he is at rest now. He does not trouble anyone any more.'

Kelly-Ann looked unconvinced and Tom butted in before she could say anything.

'Couldn't we find the owners of the house in Nairobi and at least talk to them?' he said. 'I mean, they never come here, do they? What do they want to keep the place for?'

Titus nodded.

'Yes, Tom. I think it is something we can do. At least in this respect there may be some help

KWS can offer. To set up a community reserve, help to look for financial backing, find sponsors, organize the infrastructure.'

He was thinking aloud. Mr Echessa was leaning forward now, tapping his knee with an approving fist at every welcome phrase.

'Financial backing, sponsors, infrastructure,' he repeated softly, relishing each word.

They were speaking too quietly now for the elders and onlookers to follow, and people began to get up and drift away, leaving the Echessas' compound in ones and twos, talking things over animatedly.

Kawira was slipping through the crowd, anxious to get home before Grace began to miss her.

'Wait for me!' called out Kelly-Ann, running after her.

Titus and Mr Echessa, their heads together, had settled into a serious discussion in Swahili, and Joseph had squatted down beside his uncle, keeping a respectful distance but following their arguments with interest.

Tom suddenly felt alone.

'Hey, Joseph,' he said. 'Let's go and see if the monkeys are still there.'

Joseph shook his head. He had picked up a stick and was writing numbers down in the dust, doing calculations under Titus's instruction.

Tom looked down the hill. Kawira and Kelly-

Ann had reached Grace's house now and Susanna, bobbing up and down in a bright yellow dress, was running out to greet them. There was no point in following them. He didn't feel like playing with toddlers and babies.

He thought again of the wounded young bull. It was horrible, horrible to imagine him being driven out by his family, to think of him being lonely and in pain.

And even when your face gets better and you get used to being on your own, he thought, things'll still be just as bad. I bet they don't do anything here about the lodge idea. They'll just go on talking and doing nothing, and one day you'll come back, and you'll get upset or something, and you'll chase someone else, and then you'll be in real trouble.

He looked over towards the forest. It was nearly midday now and the sun was high. The sky had paled in the intense light but the trees at the edge of the forest were a dark cool green. They seemed to invite him.

Tom stood indecisively, not knowing what to do. He had stopped listening to the men's conversation which was half in English and half in Swahili, but suddenly Mr Echessa smacked his palms together and said with satisfaction, 'You have agreed on one thing then, for the short term, that at least you will shoot this troublesome bull elephant for us, before he can return to terrorize us again.'

Titus nodded.

'Yes. We agree to that. He's clearly out of control. He could be a serious danger to you. We'll get some of the farmers to help Daniel track him down later on. He'll be on his own. It shouldn't be too difficult.'

Tom felt his blood run cold.

'No!' he burst out passionately. 'You can't! He's been wounded, that's all, and he's leaving his family. He's . . . he's upset. He'll get over it if you give him time.'

'Tom—' began Titus.

'He could easily have killed us, but he didn't. He could have trampled Kawira and gone on chasing that man, but he stopped short every time. Give him a chance. You've got to give him a chance!'

'Tom, listen.' Titus's eyes were understanding, but his voice was grave. 'There are people here, old folks, little kids. They have to live. How would you like it, eh? To suffer danger every day of your life? To see your food crops being torn up and trampled? We're going back to Nairobi, we will be safe in our houses, but these people, because of the elephants, they will face starvation.'

Tom stared blindly at him, feeling tears prickling inside his eyelids.

'I know, I know,' he said. 'But it's all wrong.'

He sniffed furiously, wiping his fist across his nose, then turned and ran out of the compound.

14

MEETING IN THE FOREST

Tom ran away from Mr Echessa's house, not wanting to see or talk to anyone. He stumbled blindly across the bare fields, in which the plants, uprooted a few days earlier by the elephants, lay crushed and dying on the ground, and stopped under the tree where yesterday they had all seen the monkeys.

The forest was no more than a few hundred metres away. Sunlight glinted on the glossy dark crowns of the great trees which shimmered gently in the soft breeze. The shade looked innocent, cool and inviting. Terrors lurked inside it, Tom knew, leopard and buffalo, giant forest hog and elephant, horn and hoof and tusk and claw, but it was calling him nevertheless. He had to go in and find the young elephant.

I can't help him, he thought, I know I can't, but if I just see him again, maybe I'll think of something.

He looked back towards the village. People were going about their daily work, chopping wood, repairing the thatch on their houses, mending fence posts. No one was working in the fields on this side of the village. It was as if they were too tired and discouraged today.

He heard a chanting song and a rhythmic clapping and saw the flash of a little yellow dress, bobbing up and down beside a pink and a blue one. Kawira and Kelly-Ann were playing a dancing game with Susanna.

No one'll miss me, he thought. I don't care if they do, anyway.

Suddenly he was afraid that someone would come out from between the houses behind him and call him back. He took off across the last stretch of open ground towards the trees.

Thick bushy undergrowth lined the edge of the forest and for a moment Tom thought that there was no way in. Then he saw an opening and ran towards it. A moment later he was walking down a narrow forest path.

He had entered a different world. There was no breeze here and the air was heavy and humid. A musty smell oozed up from the damp earth, but a few steps on a powerful scent, wafting from some unseen flower, almost made him sneeze. Sunlight penetrated the canopy overhead in a few places where a giant tree had fallen or been felled, but otherwise the shade was unbroken.

He walked a few paces into the forest then stopped, waiting for his eyes to adjust to the dimness, assessing the bushes on either side of him in case something was hiding there, watching him, nostrils flared, ready to charge or leap.

He heard nothing frightening, no rustles or growls, no pattering of hoofs. Above the continuous drone of crickets was a high-pitched twittering from dozens of unseen birds and a deeper musical hooting. He peered up into the branches of the tree overhead and saw a black bird with an improbably huge curved bill, its head cocked on one side, staring at him intelligently.

He felt a little bolder. The track was clearly marked. People obviously came and went this way. He walked on.

It was hot now. The forest was strangely stuffy, oddly alive. Butterflies like enormous bows of white, blue and orange ribbon floated around him, and ants the length of his little toe scurried about the forest floor.

He felt something running down his back and twisted his arm round to slap at it, then realized it was a trickle of sweat.

He felt discouraged.

It's impossible to find anything in here, he thought. He could be a few metres from here and I wouldn't see him with all these trees. Anyway, he's probably miles away by now.

The floor of the forest was rising more steeply and, looking up, Tom could see that the track meandered on to the top of a rise.

I'll just go up this bit, he thought. Maybe I'll be able to see better from up there.

He went on as fast as he could, concentrating on the path, trying not to slip on a loose stone, or snap a twig, or make any noise at all.

He reached the top of the rise and stopped, a little out of breath. He turned and looked back. It was no easier to make out anything up here than it had been down below. The trees and undergrowth made it impossible to see any distance at all. He peered uncertainly up the path.

There was a dip in the ground a little further on, and water had been seeping onto it out of a nearby rocky outcrop. Tom could see some kind of print in the mud. He ran up to it and found himself looking down at the perfect shape of an elephant's foot. A dry leaf had been balancing on the edge of it but the slight breeze that Tom had stirred up made it topple over into the centre of the print.

It's totally fresh, thought Tom. He must have come this way hardly any time ago.

His heart skipped a beat and his stomach lurched. He looked round cautiously, hardly daring to breathe, but the forest was as still and quiet as it had been before. With his whole body tensed and every sense alert, Tom crept on down the path. There was no mud here but he could see the faint marks of the elephant's feet, the same grey round shapes in the dust.

A giant tree had fallen across the old track, and a new track had been made around it. Tom paused, looking across the huge dead trunk, scanning the forest in front of him.

It was only a tiny sound that made him turn his head, the merest tremor of a heavy foot treading on the ground, but there, over to the right of him and no more than fifty metres away, half obscured by the undergrowth, stood an elephant. His head was turned away, but Tom could see that his trunk was raised, the tip feeling its way up the tree beside him, and that his ears were flapping restlessly, sending up clouds of dust.

Tom felt a kick of adrenalin running through him and though he was standing absolutely still his mind began to race.

The elephant seemed unaware of him. He was moving about irritably, worrying now at the tree trunk with the tips of his tusks. Tom eased his head round carefully to look back down the path. Should he risk retracing his steps? Should he duck down behind the fallen tree and wait for the elephant to go away?

The elephant turned his head a little further towards him and slowly flapped his ears again. Instinct told Tom to run, to hare back down the path, to get far away as fast as he could. Common sense told him to watch and wait, to be quiet and still, to avoid attracting the elephant's attention and at all costs not to startle him.

He began to creep slowly and cautiously along the trunk towards the far end where the upended roots made good protective cover. He moved springily on tensed calves, keeping a watchful eye on the elephant and glancing down to avoid snapping a tell-tale twig or catching himself on the thorns of the trailing vines that were already smothering the fallen tree.

He was almost behind the fan of old roots when he stopped suddenly, realizing that he was about to brush past a clump of the biggest nettles he had ever seen with leaves the size of saucers and prickles a centimetre long.

He looked up again. The elephant was tossing his head now, waving aloft a tuft of grass held in a coil of his trunk. Tom could see clearly a dark wound on his cheek, below his eye.

It's him. It's *him*! he thought exultantly.

The elephant was looking across to a point beyond Tom, still clearly unaware of him. All at once he rumbled, a deep sound that rippled through the forest like the purr of a gigantic cat. The sound brought back to Tom the full terror of the day before, the screaming trumpeting and wild charges, the thunder of enormous feet, the slashing of ivories. Panic welled up inside him and, abandoning all caution, he darted round to the far side of the clump of nettles and bolted behind a bush, desperate to get out of sight.

I was crazy to come in here, he thought. I shouldn't have done it.

He stood for a moment, trying to control his noisy breathing, listening with straining ears for any sound that might tell him what the elephant was doing. Then he heard the long low rumbling sound again. The elephant was calling. The noise went on for a while, then it stopped and all he could hear was the chattering of the birds and the crickets' rasping song.

His fright had made him shake all over. He couldn't think clearly any more. He didn't know what to do.

He was convinced all of a sudden that something was just ahead of him, on the other side of the bush. He imagined that the elephant had come towards him on silent feet, that he was standing even now only two or three metres away, his trunk raised like a whip, his tusks poised, ready to slash at him. The suspense was unbearable. Gingerly, wincing at every rustle he made, he leaned forward, parted the branches of the bush and looked out.

The elephant had hardly moved. He was standing in the same place, his head a little lower, the tip of his trunk, out of sight to Tom, fiddling with something on the ground.

Then, as Tom watched, his head jerked up as if he'd just heard or seen something.

Tom, sure he'd been scented at last, let the branches spring gently back together.

What do I do? What on earth do I do? he thought frantically, looking behind and all around him.

He was just about to make a break for it – he'd almost decided to dash back onto the path and take his chance of racing the elephant back to the village – when he heard another rumble, even deeper, coming from some way away. It was followed by a kind of snorting noise and a heavy rustle of shaking bushes.

There's more of them! thought Tom. They're coming this way!

In the dense suffocating air it was impossible to tell which direction the sounds were coming from. Not knowing which way to turn, his heart thudding painfully in his chest, he bent down and crept right under the lowest branches of the bush. It was hardly a safe shelter but at least he was out of sight.

He found he could see, too. Through gaps in the leaves he still had a good view of the elephant, *his* elephant, who was walking slowly out from the deep shade where he'd been resting towards a small sunlit clearing further up the path. His trunk was raised as if in greeting.

Then Tom saw the others. First, down the path towards him came another elephant, a gigantic bull, the biggest animal Tom had ever seen. He walked gently, almost silently, his great trunk swinging from side to side with each rolling step, his ears lying peacefully beside his head. Behind him came another and another.

Tom sat as if turned to stone. His survival depended, he knew, on staying hidden, on keeping these vast creatures ignorant of his presence. Paradoxically, he was a little less afraid now that there were several of them. His elephant had seemed jumpy and jittery, as if he might lose his temper easily and take it out on whoever got in his way. But the new arrivals looked calm and unhurried, as if they were out for a pleasant stroll in the woods, relaxing with a crowd of friends.

The group of elephants came abreast of the clearing and caught sight of Tom's bull. At once they halted and turned towards him. Tom's bull trumpeted once, almost meekly, then trotted across to the biggest elephant who towered over him, his gigantic curved tusks lowered unthreateningly. Gently, almost timidly, the young bull lifted his trunk and touched the other's face with the tip, moving it delicately over the great bull's massive forehead. The big elephant lifted his in turn, and the two of them coiled their trunks together, wreathing them in a sinuous friendly greeting.

Tom had forgotten his fear. He had pulled the branches back again so that he could see more easily, sensing that the elephants were more interested in each other than they would be in him. He was watching in wonder, marvelling at them, admiring their strength and gentleness, trying to understand what they were communicating to each other.

They're greeting each other, he thought. It almost looks as if they've met before. Maybe they have, and now they're checking my elephant out properly. They're all bulls, so perhaps they'll let him go off with them and be in their gang.

The young wounded bull was still nervous. He shied back suddenly as another elephant came too close and flapped his ears aggressively.

'Don't!' breathed Tom. 'Don't mess it up! Don't you understand?'

The outstretched trunk of the second elephant gently touched the wounded bull's face in greeting. The wounded bull seemed to relax, and stood quietly as the others congregated round him.

Yes, that's good, make friends, urged Tom silently.

One of the smallest elephants, who was still larger than Tom's bull, had been moving restlessly round the outside of the group, tossing his head as if seeking attention. Tom's elephant turned towards him and, as if answering a challenge, curled back his trunk and raised his tusks.

'No!' Tom muttered. 'Don't mess it up. Don't

fight! Just go with them. Follow them. It's your only chance! Please!'

The other bull, with a shrill trumpet, laid his own trunk on Tom's bull's forehead and began to push. The two of them strained against each other for a moment or two, then Tom's bull, made cautious perhaps by the still painful wound in his cheek, broke away snorting a little. He backed off, flapping his ears gently and lowering his head.

The big bull was already leading the way out of the clearing, turning back up the path towards the heart of the forest. One by one, the others followed him. Tom's elephant stood looking after them and for a long moment Tom was afraid that he wouldn't follow, that he'd go the other way, back towards the fields and the village, straight into the path of the trackers and Daniel's gun.

Then he shook himself and, almost skittishly for such a heavy creature, he gave a little snort and cantered up the path after the others, dropping his pace to match their leisurely amble as he fell in at the end of the line.

For a long moment, after they'd disappeared from sight, Tom stayed still. He felt as if a knot that had been tied up inside him had come undone, and a strong, good feeling, a kind of satisfaction, was running out from the centre of his body along his veins.

You'll be all right now, he thought, standing

up and firmly sweeping a couple of exploring ants off his leg.

He stepped confidently out onto the path again, sure that the forest held no more dangers for him today. He walked slowly, alive to the intense life around him in a way he hadn't been before.

He saw now that it was beautiful, that everywhere he looked something miraculous was happening. The huge leaves, trembling gently on the fine stalks by the path, were the most brilliant green he had ever seen. The vines, snaking up and around the smooth silvery trunks of the trees, were as strong as hawsers. The primrose wings of the butterfly that was sucking nectar from a great white flower by the path, were delicately veined with black.

For some reason he thought of Mum and the baby.

It must be scary having a baby, he said to himself. I hope they're OK, I really, really do.

He was glad all of a sudden that he was a boy and not an elephant. There was no need for him to run off into a forest, or anywhere else for that matter, and live alone. He'd got a family and he was going back to it. That was where he belonged.

15

TOM LAYS A FALSE TRAIL

Tom emerged out into the open from the cover of the trees. It had taken him ages to get back. He'd thought he was lost once or twice, and he'd forced himself to go slowly, to look around carefully and remember what he'd seen on his way in.

The light outside the forest was so strong that it almost dazzled him and he shaded his eyes to look down towards the village. The girls were out of sight now, and Titus and Joseph, he supposed, were still talking things over with Mr Echessa. The only people he could see were a group of five or six farmers coming across the fields towards him from the upper end of the village. Daniel, spruce in his khaki and brown camouflage uniform, was with them, his gun slung casually over his shoulder.

Tom halted, shock rippling through him. He'd thought there'd be more time. He'd never imagined that Daniel and the trackers would go after the young bull so soon.

Before he'd had time to think things out properly, he changed direction and veered off to meet them.

'Tom! Where have you been?' Daniel called out when he was still some way away. Tom saw that he was frowning. 'Everyone's looking for you.'

'Sorry,' said Tom. 'I . . . I was looking at butterflies. Inside the forest. I suppose I forgot the time.'

The farmers sucked in their breath through their teeth and shook their heads disapprovingly.

'It is too dangerous,' Daniel said severely. 'Mr Musau will not let you do such a thing. No one should go into the forest alone. That elephant, he has too much pain from his wound. He can attack you – Bam! Bam! Just like that.'

'Oh, there weren't any elephants around,' said Tom, as casually as he could.

'Buffalo even,' Daniel went on. 'A buffalo alone is the most dangerous of all the animals. He is so angry. He goes so fast, he sees you, he charges, so quick to twist and turn. He will kill you for sure.'

Tom nodded placatingly.

'Yeah, you're right. I know. I'm really sorry. You're not going in there yourself, are you?'

'We're looking for the young bull. We have to try and find him before nightfall.'

'The young bull elephant?' said Tom, as casually as he could. 'I can show you where he is.'

He was thinking rapidly, a plan forming in his head.

'You have seen him?' Daniel clicked his tongue. 'Tom, you are lucky you are not dead by now.'

'No, it was OK, I wasn't close to him. I saw him from a distance. I heard him too.'

The farmers looked at each other doubtfully.

'Where?' said Daniel. 'We didn't hear anything.'

'No, you wouldn't have done,' said Tom. 'He was a long way away, beyond the hill. I was lucky to catch a glimpse of him ... er ... between the trees. He was going that way.'

He pointed in the opposite direction from where the elephants had gone.

'You could not be sure,' said Daniel. 'It might be another elephant. There are many in the forest.'

Tom shrugged.

'Yeah, maybe. But I saw his wound, you know, that sore place under his eye.'

Daniel, unconvinced, had already begun to walk on. Tom racked his brains.

'I only saw one other big animal in there and it wasn't an elephant,' he said desperately.

The farmers were following Daniel, but the last two turned back.

'What? What kind of animal?' asked one of the men, turning round.

'I didn't see it very clearly.' Tom was inventing furiously. 'It was kind of black and it had really big horns.' He screwed up his eyes, trying to remember the buffalo he'd seen in Nairobi National Park. 'The horns – they were like a kind of helmet, you know, meeting across the middle of his head and sort of curving round the side.'

'*Nyati!* Buffalo!' the two farmers said, looking at each other. One of them shouted something to Daniel and the others who had gone ahead. They came back and the group of men stood in a ring, looking down at Tom.

Tom felt a blush rise in his cheeks and hoped that the men would think he was just feeling shy.

'It was there, just inside the forest. I . . . I think there were two of them. The other one was higher up the track.'

The farmers talked for a moment in Swahili, then one of them clapped Tom on the shoulder.

'This one is a good boy. We will look for the elephant tomorrow.'

They turned and began to walk back down the hill towards a stand of trees on the far side of the village.

Daniel looked at Tom curiously.

'I haven't seen a buffalo here for many years,' he said. 'You're sure that is what you saw?'

'Yes.' Tom's eyes were bent on the path as they walked slowly back towards the village. 'It couldn't have been anything else, could it?'

He broke away from Daniel with relief and ran the last few metres to Grace's house. He came round the side wall and almost bumped into Kawira.

She looked up at him shyly.

'They are looking for you,' she said. 'They are saying you must go now.'

'Oh.'

He felt strange at the idea of saying goodbye. He'd been in this village for less than twenty-four hours but it felt like years and years.

Out of the corner of his eye, he noticed Kawira's slim dark hand twisting in and out of a fold of her faded blue dress. He wanted to say something to her and cleared his throat.

Kelly-Ann came out of Grace's house.

'Tom! We thought we'd lost you,' she said. 'Thought we'd have to go without you.' She came up to them and twined her arms round Kawira's waist. 'Me and Kawira are going to write to each other, aren't we, Kawira? We're going to be pen pals.'

An unreadable expression crossed Kawira's face. Then she looked up, caught Tom's eye and smiled.

'When the lodge is ready, you will come back and see how it is with us?' she said.

'Yes,' said Tom. 'I will. I'd love to come back. I'm going to bring my mum and dad. It'd be great helping to repair it. You know, clearing out all the leaves and stuff. It would be brilliant fun.'

Titus and Mr Echessa appeared, still talking

earnestly. Mr Echessa was punctuating every sentence with large arm movements, nodding his head vociferously and spreading out his hands. Titus saw Tom and his face lit up.

'Tom, I was getting worried about you. Where have you been?'

Before Tom could think of an answer, Joseph ran up to him.

'It's so great,' he said. 'They've been thinking about so many things. How to persuade the farmers, how to get the land—' He broke off. 'Hey! Where were you, anyway? I came to look for you. I couldn't find you anywhere.'

'I'll tell you.' Tom grabbed his sleeve and pulled him aside. He didn't want the girls to know about how he'd seen the elephant. He didn't want anyone to know, except for Joseph. 'I went into the forest. On my own.'

'What?' Joseph opened his eyes wide and his eyebrows shot up towards his hair. 'Are you crazy? It's dangerous in there. Titus will beat the hell out of you if he finds out.'

'Yeah, but he's not going to, is he?' Tom grinned at him. 'Listen, Joseph. You won't believe this. I saw him. He was there.'

'Who? Who was there? You are so mysterious, Tom. You saw Elvis? John Lennon? An axe murderer? The dead *mzungu*?'

'No, you idiot. The elephant. The wounded one who chased us.'

Joseph stared at him.

'You're mad,' he said with conviction. 'You followed a rogue elephant into the forest on your own? You have a death wish. Does your family know about this?'

'No, no, honestly. Listen. You saw him yesterday with the females. You know how Titus said they get driven away from their families and have to find other males and kind of get into a gang? Well, I saw it. I mean I saw him go off with them.'

Joseph shook his head, mystified.

'What are you talking about?'

'I tell you, I saw him. I knew it was him because of that hole in his cheek. He was on his own, and restless, you know, as if you'd only have to click your fingers and he'd have a go at you again. I was dead scared, I can tell you. I hid behind an old dead tree.'

He stopped, remembering it all again.

'Go on,' said Joseph.

'So then a bunch of other male elephants came down the track and they saw our elephant. It was as if they'd known each other before, and they were sort of deciding to make friends. It was so amazing. They touched each other's faces with their trunks, and one of the young ones had a kind of play wrestle with him.'

'Like this, you mean.'

Joseph got Tom's arm in an armlock.

'Get off.' Tom pulled himself free. 'Then they all turned around and walked off up the path into the forest, and our one stayed back for a moment. Honestly, it was so incredible, as if he was kind of making his mind up. Then he followed them. I reckon he'll be all right now.'

Joseph was shaking his head.

'Tom, I don't believe this. There was a whole crowd of male elephants, and you were alone in the forest, and you just sat there watching them?'

'Yes. I was behind a bush. I could see everything.'

'You weren't scared?'

'Course I was scared. But it was so brilliant too, being close to them and everything.'

'Yeah. You're lucky, Tom.' He shook his head. 'And you really think our wounded one, he's gone off with the others? I hope you're right. I hope he'll be OK. But there's something you don't know. Daniel went into the forest with some farmers just now. He said if they see him again they're going to shoot him.'

Tom grinned.

'Yes, I do know. I met them. Told them I'd seen him, but pointed them in the wrong direction. Then I said I'd seen a buffalo. They believed me. They said they'd leave it till tomorrow. I guess our bull will be miles away with all his new mates by then.'

Joseph looked at him admiringly.

'Eh, man,' he said. 'You are a man.'

Titus had started walking off towards the jeep.

'Come!' he called over his shoulder. 'It's time to go.'

The whole village had come out to see them off. There was a crowd around the jeep shaking hands with Titus and waving at Kelly-Ann as she climbed into the front seat.

Tom opened the rear door to climb in himself, and saw Grace holding Eliud, his head cuddled down into her shoulder. He tickled Eliud under the ear, and Eliud wriggled and opened his mouth to smile, letting a long dribble run down his chin.

'Goodbye,' said Grace. 'Come again. You are always welcome.'

'Thank you.' Tom looked past her to wave at Kawira. 'I'll see you again. I'll come back.'

He didn't look round at the crowd as the jeep bumped away down the track. His eyes were fixed on the distant forest. Somewhere among those dark green trees his elephant was walking with his soft deliberate tread, following his new friends to safety.

Titus swung the jeep round a corner, heading off the main track.

'Where are we going?' asked Joseph.

Titus changed to overdrive gear and the jeep's engine revved noisily.

'I want to see this house of yours. If KWS are

going to support this project, we've got to know if it's going to work.'

'I'm not going back in there again,' said Kelly-Ann. 'There's snakes. Anyway, I bet Kawira was right. I bet that snake we saw was really a wicked spirit.'

Titus frowned.

'I don't like to hear you say such a thing, Kelly-Ann,' he said, with unusual sharpness. 'That's the way so many animals have suffered from human beings. Just because we don't like snakes, we say that they're evil, or demons, or spirits, so that we have an excuse to kill them. And hyenas, OK, they're not beautiful animals, but they're per-secuted sometimes because people tell all these spirit stories. It's bad to have such superstitions.'

'They did that to wolves in Europe once,' said Tom. 'Called people werewolves and hunted real wolves to death.'

'Yeah, well, I didn't know. I mean, it could have been a spirit, couldn't it?' said Kelly-Ann.

'No,' said Titus.

'Er . . . no,' said Tom.

'Well . . . no,' said Joseph.

They had all spoken at the same time and burst out laughing.

The lane was too narrow now for the jeep and Titus put on the brakes.

'We'll walk from here,' he said. 'Tom and

Joseph, lead the way. Kelly-Ann, stay with the car if you like.'

Kelly-Ann sighed.

'No,' she said. 'You win, you lot, as usual. I'll come with you, I suppose.'

16
A SURPRISE FOR TOM

They walked up the short overgrown track to the old *mzungu* house and stood looking up at it again.

'It's open at the back,' Tom told Titus.

Titus nodded.

'Stay here, you kids,' he said. 'I won't be long.' He began to force his way through the undergrowth at the side of the house.

Tom felt secretly relieved. He hadn't wanted to admit it, but the idea of seeing the snake again had given him a cold feeling in the pit of his stomach.

He sat down on a branch that had fallen off a huge tree and half listened to Kelly-Ann and Joseph, who were arguing about the name the lodge should have when it opened.

'Elephant View, I told you,' Kelly-Ann was saying. 'Then people will know they're going to see elephants and get a fabulous view as well.'

'But you can't see elephants from here,' objected Joseph. 'Anyway, the name should have a Swahili word in it. Ndovo Adventure Lodge, maybe.'

Tom blocked their voices out. He was imagining Kawira, a few years older, standing behind a reception desk in a uniform the same colour as the blue dress she'd been wearing, smiling shyly at the guests and taking their keys down for them from the board behind her head.

Titus came back a few minutes later.

'This place is extraordinary,' he said. 'Exceptional. There's a great possibility here, ideal conditions. The village people are keen. The site's outstanding. I'm going to get to work on this as soon as I get back to Nairobi.'

He began to stride back down the track towards the jeep. The others followed him.

'We've got a name for the hotel,' said Kelly-Ann, running alongside him. 'Elephant View.'

Joseph rolled his eyes.

'No, Ndovo Adventure,' he said.

Titus put a hand on each of their shoulders and looked back at Tom, who was following a few paces behind.

'I think it should be called Discovery Lodge,' he said. 'It was you who discovered it, after all.'

They reached the jeep and climbed into it, Tom in the front this time, and Joseph and Kelly-Ann in the back. Titus let out the brake and they began on the long bumpy ride down from the slopes of Mount Kenya.

Tom leaned out of the window, looking with awe at the vast landscape of Africa unfolding in front of him as the jeep lurched down towards the tarmac road that would take them first through the rolling foothills across the plain and then back to the dust and traffic of Nairobi. He bent forward and tapped Titus on the shoulder.

'Please,' he said, 'we don't have to tell my mum and dad everything that happened, do we? It's just that they don't . . . I mean they might get sort of worried and . . .'

He stopped.

'And not let you go off without them again?' Titus turned round and grinned at him. 'I wouldn't blame them at all.' He changed gear and the Land Rover roared loudly. 'It's all right,' he said, raising his voice above the noise of the engine. 'They have enough to worry about with a new baby coming. We don't have to trouble them with all our adventures.'

Tom sat back in his seat and let the countryside roll by. He'd hardly spoken a word on the way here, and he didn't want to talk much now. Inside, though, he felt completely different. He'd been angry and defensive and guilty then. Now he felt calm and loving and strong.

The cool thin air of high altitude was quickly giving way to the heavier, warmer air of the plain. The forest seemed miles away already, floating high above him, as if its strange plants and mysterious sounds and smells belonged to a different, distant world. Tom could hardly believe it was really there at all.

They reached the tarmac road. The jeep speeded up. The familiar sights and sounds of Kenya – the minibuses crammed with people, the trucks ferrying export vegetables to the airport, the small roadside shops – flashed past Tom. In a few hours time he'd be at home.

He was beginning to feel worried now. What if something awful had happened to Mum? Would he get the blame? And even if she was OK, would she still be angry with him?

A knot of anxiety began to tighten in his stomach.

It was nearly nightfall when at last the jeep turned in through the Wilkinsons' gate and pulled up outside the door. Tom wrenched the jeep door open, tumbled out and ran round the side of the house to the back door. He burst into the kitchen.

It was empty. He ran into the sitting room. His dad was sitting on the sofa, shoes off, tie loosened, slumped in a deep sleep.

'Dad! Dad!' said Tom, shaking him. 'I'm back. What happened? How's Mum?'

Simon Wilkinson woke with a jerk and sat up groggily, shaking his head to clear the mistiness out of his eyes.

'Oh hello, Tom. What a fright you gave me! Had a good time? See any elephants? What have you done with Kelly-Ann?'

'Murdered her,' said Tom. 'Come on, Dad, where's Mum?'

'In hospital.' Simon stretched and yawned. Then he saw the agonized look on Tom's face and grinned. 'No, it's OK. She's fine. So's your little brother.'

'What? *What*? The baby came? It's a boy?'

Tom could hardly take it in. He was awash with a mixture of relief, excitement and anxiety.

'Yes. Isn't it brilliant? Another boy in the family!' Simon reached up to punch Tom joyfully on the shoulder. 'We'll be able to play three-a-side football.' He leaned forward to the low table by the sofa and felt the half-empty cup that was sitting on it. 'This is cold. I must have dropped off. I need another coffee. Come into the kitchen. I'll tell you all about it.'

Tom grabbed his arm. The others would be in the kitchen by now. He wanted to ask Simon something first.

'The baby's miles too early, isn't he?' he said. 'Is he going to be OK?'

Simon nodded.

'Not that early. Three weeks. Yeah, he'll be all right. He's a whopper for thirty-seven weeks. Greedy little blighter, too.'

He was grinning proudly.

'But what about Mum? I mean, it was the snake and all that that got her going, wasn't it? I've got to tell you what really happened. It was all my fault in a way. You see, I . . .'

Simon got to his feet, put his arm round Tom's shoulder and gave him a little shake.

'No, it wasn't all your fault. She told me about it. Said you'd had a row. OK, she was cross with you at the time but she felt bad about it too, foisting that little madam on you and everything.'

'She's not a madam really,' said Tom. 'She's a bit kind of pathetic in a way. Anyway, never mind her. I just wanted to know if – I mean, the baby wouldn't have come as early if Mum hadn't had such a fright, would he? I mean, there might be things wrong with him because of that.'

'No,' said Simon positively. 'They've done loads of tests. They think he's fine. The doctor said her blood pressure was way up anyway. She might have needed to go in and have him induced early. Anyway, she's fine now, and so's the baby, so stop worrying about it, OK?'

Tom gave a shuddering sigh.

'Oh Dad, I felt awful. I really, really did.'

'Nah, cheer up.' Simon was walking over to the kitchen door. 'We all make mistakes. Don't worry about it. Mum's not bothered about that now. Anyway, we're going to be too busy celebrating to worry about anything else.'

'Were you there?' said Tom. 'When he was born, I mean. Was it awful? It hurts a lot, doesn't it?'

'I wouldn't know.' Simon paused at the door to look back at him. 'Yes,' he went on, dropping his joky voice. 'Yes, I bet it does, but I was with her you know, all the way through, when all three of you were born, and she's so brave and calm you wouldn't believe it. She's great, your mum is. A real fighter.' He winked at Tom. 'Mind you, when it comes to procreation, I'd rather stick with the bit I do and leave the rest to her.'

'Dad!' said Tom, furiously embarrassed, but Simon had gone into the kitchen.

'Hi Kelly-Ann, hi Joseph. How was Meru?' Tom heard him say. 'Hello, Titus. I hope the kids behaved themselves. Can't tell you how grateful I am. There was a real old dust-up here. Debbie went into labour. Come through into the sitting room and I'll tell you all about it. Wait, let me get you a drink first. You can celebrate with me. You are now looking at a proud father of three!'

Tom spent the rest of the evening in a kind of daze. He felt gloriously happy and completely exhausted at the same time.

He was suddenly starving, too.

'Here,' said Simon vaguely, when Joseph and Titus had finally said goodbye and gone back next door. 'I suppose you two are hungry. There's stuff in the fridge I think. What do you want to eat?'

'I don't care. Anything,' said Tom, flinging the fridge door open and surveying the various mysterious packets on the shelves inside it.

'I wouldn't mind a vegetarian pizza, if you've got one,' said Kelly-Ann anxiously.

'Might be some in the freezer,' said Tom. 'Mum made some pizzas last week. I'll look.'

He went into the little room off the kitchen and came back triumphant.

'There you go. One salami and pepper, one cheese and mushroom.'

'Mushroom? I hate mushrooms,' said Kelly-Ann. Haven't you got one that's just cheese?'

'No,' said Tom shortly. 'Do you want one, Dad?'

'No thanks,' said Simon. 'I ate on the way home from hospital, after I'd seen your mum.'

'Have you fed Tiger?' said Tom, looking round for his little cat.

'What? Oh damn, I forgot,' said Simon guiltily. 'She must still be outside.'

Tom opened the back door and Tiger marched in at once, her tail held high. She began to weave herself around Tom's feet, miaowing fiercely. Tom opened the fridge again. There was some cat food ready in a bowl. He spooned some out into Tiger's dish. She ate greedily. He watched her with satisfaction.

He suddenly realized that he was missing his sister.

'Where's Bella?' he said.

'Next door, with Sarah,' said Simon. 'She loves it there. Sarah and Afra spoil her rotten if you ask me.'

He tried to take the pizzas out of Tom's hands.

'It's OK, Dad, I'll do it. I know how,' said Tom. He turned on the oven and put the salami pizza in. 'You look really shattered.'

'I am,' said Simon feelingly. 'I was up all the night before last and didn't get much sleep last night either.'

There was a knock on the outside door. Kelly-Ann ran over to open it, and Afra came in with Kiksy crouching low on her shoulder, his enormous saucer-like eyes surveying the room as if everything in it came as a great surprise.

'Kiksy! You're better!' said Tom.

Afra grinned.

'He's fine, aren't you, little guy?' She stroked Kiksy's soft back with her free hand, and the bushbaby chattered lovingly at her. 'I took him to the vet but he said not to worry. It was something he ate, like I thought. He's been quite well since this morning. Congratulations, Tom. You have a little brother! Wow! I can't wait to see him.'

Tom smiled.

'Me too.'

He didn't know what else to say.

'How was Meru?' said Afra. 'You had a good time?'

'Meru? We didn't ever get to . . .' began Kelly-Ann, but Tom silenced her with a look. Dad was looking battered enough tonight. The story, or an edited version of it, could wait till tomorrow.

Chimes sounded through the house.

'Someone's at the front door,' said Simon.

'Mum! It'll be my mum!' cried Kelly-Ann, running out into the hall after him.

'Was she awful?' Afra said sympathetically.

He made a horrible face.

'Look at me. I am the saint who went away with Kelly-Ann and didn't strangle her.'

Afra chuckled.

'You're a saint? How come I never noticed before?'

'She's kind of helpless,' Tom went on. 'I don't know. Needs looking after or something. Haven't you seen Joseph? Didn't he tell you what happened?'

'No.' Afra shook her head. 'He was starting to tell me when Sarah came in. Then he just clammed up.'

Tom nodded.

'Just as well. He didn't want to drop Titus in it, I expect. Sarah would have a fit if she knew what we'd been doing.'

'Tell me then!' Afra was exasperated. 'Don't keep me hanging about for ever!'

'You're not going to believe it. It was the most incredible weekend I've ever had in my whole life. For a start, we never even got as far as Meru. This ranger, Daniel . . .'

Footsteps sounded outside the door and Simon and Kelly-Ann came back into the kitchen with Kelly-Ann's mum, thin and deeply sunburnt, clacking in after them in her white high-heeled shoes. She was laughing up at Simon, flicking back her big puffs of blond hair, making her dangling earrings jangle.

'Oh it was wonderful of you, Simon, just so wonderful,' she was saying. 'I mean, if I'd *known*, of course! Poor Debbie. Just like that! Ever so sudden, wasn't it?'

Kelly-Ann was tugging at her arm.

'Mum! Mum, I nearly got done by a raving mad elephant. He charged us. I was that scared. It was like—'

Her mother pulled her arm away.

'Not now, Kelly-Ann. I'm talking.' She turned back to Simon. 'Fancy your friend taking her off to – where was it? Meru? What did you say his name was again?'

'Titus,' said Simon. 'Titus Musau.'

'What a funny name. Do I know him?'

'I don't know,' said Simon. 'He works for the Kenya Wildlife Service.'

Kelly-Ann's mother took hold of her daughter's arm and a strange look crossed her face.

'You mean he's an African?' she said. 'How very – I mean, you let Tom and Kelly-Ann go off on their own with an African?'

Simon's face went stiff.

'Haven't you noticed?' he said. 'We're living in Africa. Most people here happen to be Africans. And of all the people I've ever met, black or white, the one I'd most like my kids to hang out with is Titus Musau.'

Kelly-Ann's mother wasn't listening. She was looking down at Kelly-Ann, who was pumping at her hand again. Tom watched anxiously. He waggled his eyebrows, trying to catch Kelly-Ann's eye.

'Listen, Mum. I'm trying to tell you,' Kelly-Ann went on. 'We didn't ever go to . . .'

She saw Tom's signalling eyebrows and stopped. He could read in her face a kind of struggle. She wanted to make a drama out of the whole thing, he could see, to get her mother's attention at last and be at the centre of a storm of outrage. He held his breath.

'It was amazing, Mum,' she said in a quieter voice. 'We went somewhere much better than Meru. Titus took us to this brilliant place – an extremely exclusive lodge.'

'Oh really? Where's that?' her mother said, her interest captured at last.

'It's called Elephant View,' said Kelly-Ann, throwing Tom a triumphant look. 'Me and Tom and Joseph and Kawira went round it on our own.'

'Who are Joseph and Kawira?' said her mother, looking bewildered.

'My friends,' said Kelly-Ann.

'Oh, what a funny little thing you are.' Her mother gave a tinkling laugh. 'Honestly, Simon, you wouldn't believe how many friends Kelly-Ann's got. I can't keep up with them all. Come on then, miss. Say goodbye and thank-you. I'm going to get you home. You'd talk the hind leg off a donkey if I let you stay here any longer. You're so full of your own stories you haven't asked me a single question about how we got on at the coast.'

She began to usher Kelly-Ann out of the door. Kelly-Ann turned and caught Tom's eye. He gave her a secret thumbs-up sign and his grateful smile was warm and broad.

'Come again, Kelly-Ann,' he said, knowing he'd regret it but meaning it all the same.

Her eyes narrowed slightly as she looked at him, then she flashed a smile back.

'OK,' she said. 'I will.'

'What's it all *about*?' demanded Afra, when at last Simon, Kelly-Ann and her mother had gone out of the room. 'I'm going to explode in a minute!'

'It's a very long story,' said Tom. 'I'll come round first thing tomorrow and tell you all about it.'

'No, you won't,' said Simon, coming back into the kitchen. 'Not unless you don't want to come to the hospital with me to see Mum and the baby.'

'Of course I do!' Something else occurred to Tom and he looked a little anxious again. 'Did you get that broken window fixed? In the baby's room?'

'Yes. The man came this morning.' Simon lifted his nose and sniffed. 'What's that smell?'

'My pizza!' Tom made a dash for the oven.

Afra grinned and stroked Kiksy, who had fluffed up his hair in fright at Tom's shout.

'I'll see you then,' she said. 'I guess I'd better go now.'

'Yeah. I'll come when I've seen Mum, and what's-his-name. What is his name, Dad?'

'I don't know.' Simon took the pizza out of Tom's hands and put it on the table. 'We haven't decided yet. You know what, Tom, the smell of that pizza's made me hungry. I think I'll do the mushroom one too. Might as well. Kelly-Ann's not going to eat it now, is she?' He hunted about in a drawer, looking for scissors. 'It beats me why your mum wrapped this thing up so you need a chainsaw to get the plastic off.'

'Bye, then,' said Afra, but Tom and Simon were too busy to notice her. She made a face at their backs and let herself out through the back door.

Although Tom was tired, he went to bed late that night. When Simon's pizza was done, he took it into the sitting room and started watching a football match on TV. Tom flopped down on the sofa beside him. They watched silently for a while.

'We saw some elephants, Dad,' said Tom at last. 'A whole family of them. There was a baby, and this young bull, he had a gash under his eyes, and he was being a bit aggressive and the others chased him off. He was so . . . so . . .'

'Goal!' shouted Simon, half rising out of his seat.

Tom gave up. He realized suddenly that he was exhausted and he pulled himself up off the sofa.

'Night, Dad,' he said.

'You're off?' said Simon, looking up from the screen. He blinked, seeming to see Tom properly. 'Sorry. I was a bit carried away. That was the best header I've seen in years. Tell me about the elephants tomorrow. You look blitzed.'

'I am,' said Tom, smiling woozily at him.

'You don't have to get up early tomorrow,' said Simon. 'We're not allowed into the hospital till eleven. I'll have to get up, worse luck. I've got to fix those dratted curtains in the baby's room. Fiddling little hooks. It'll take for-ever.'

'Wake me up and I'll give you a hand,' said Tom. 'Night, Dad.'

'Night, son. Nice to have you back.'

Tom slept a deep dreamless sleep all night long, and when he woke a shaft of sunlight, dappled through the tree, was slicing in through the chink in his curtains. He lay for a while, looking at the elephant poster on the opposite wall as if seeing it for the first time.

The door opened and Simon poked his head into the room.

'Awake at last!' he said. 'I thought you'd sleep all day. Well, are you coming to the hospital, or aren't you?'

Tom leapt out of bed.

'Try and stop me.'

'I've been trying to *wake* you for the last couple of hours. Got any advice for next time? I tried shaking you, calling you, tickling your toes – nothing worked.'

'Sorry, Dad.' Tom was hauling on his clothes. 'What about the curtains? Do you want to put them up before we go?'

'Oh, I finished doing that hours ago,' said Simon. 'Here, don't forget to wash your face and brush your hair. First impressions are important, after all, and you never know, your little brother might be fussy about that kind of thing.'

It took longer than Tom had expected to drive to the hospital, and by the time they arrived he was feeling edgy with excitement. Simon parked the car, and the two of them walked in through the big double doors, stepping aside for a group of young doctors in white coats who were talking eagerly in Swahili.

Tom wasn't used to hospitals, and the smell of antiseptic and the sight of the nurses in their starchy uniforms made him feel nervous as he followed his father down the long corridor. Simon stopped at the very last door and pushed it open.

There was only one bed in the room. Debbie was propped up in it, looking down at a bundle she was cradling in her arms. Tom caught a glimpse of a mop of spiky black hair, then Debbie looked up and smiled at him.

'Hi, big brother,' she said.

Tom tiptoed round to the side of the bed, feeling clumsy and too big, afraid of blundering into things, or touching something he shouldn't. Debbie put her face up for a kiss and he leaned over carefully and kissed her cheek.

'Hi, Mum.' He hesitated. He wanted to say sorry before he lost his courage, but he didn't know how to. She was looking up at him, smiling fondly. 'Look,' he blurted out, 'I'm really, really sorry. I never should have said that to you, or been so bad-tempered and all that. I've been so worried about you, in case it was me that made it all go wrong.'

She disengaged her spare hand from under the baby and gently pinched his chin.

'It's all right, love. Don't worry about it. Everything's fine. I was on a short fuse too.'

The baby moved, his tiny mouth began to work and one little hand started waving in the air. Tom looked down, studying him for the first time. The baby's face was red and crumpled, and there was a crease in his forehead as if he was frowning.

'Isn't he beautiful?' said Debbie.

'Yes,' said Tom politely, but he didn't think the baby was beautiful at all. He was ugly in fact, although Tom could see that he was sort of fascinating as well. He looked tiny and soft, but strong too. He was a real person.

'Here,' said Debbie. 'Take him.'

She held him up to Tom. With infinite care, he took the bundle and held it as if it was a piece of rare porcelain.

'He's so light,' he said wonderingly. 'And warm. And he smells kind of sweet.'

He felt a new kind of love, a melting feeling, unlike anything he'd known before.

'What are we going to call him?' he said.

Simon and Debbie exchanged looks.

'We can't make our minds up,' said Debbie. 'Dad wants Robert, but I like James.'

'Robert. James.' Tom tried them both out. 'Rob. Jim. Jimmy.' He smiled at Debbie. 'I vote for Jimmy. Look at him. Doesn't he look like a Jimmy to you?'

Simon took the baby out of Tom's arms.

'Give him here. I haven't had a go yet.' He pulled the blanket away from the baby's head. 'Let's look at you then.' He studied the baby's face. 'Yes, OK, Tom. I guess you're right. Jimmy it is.'

Debbie patted the bed, inviting Tom to sit down beside her.

'How did you get on in Meru, love? How did it go with Joseph and Kelly-Ann and everything?'

A dozen pictures flashed through Tom's mind: a skinny, tense little girl in a pink dress; a bull elephant, his trunk raised, charging towards him on thundering feet; the face of a woman in the firelight desperately willing her children to be silent; a young girl in a blue dress standing in the soft lamplight in an open doorway; a ring of African farmers squatting round the tall handsome figure of Titus Musau; an old stone house, half lost under a riot of roses; a troop of black and white monkeys, flinging themselves from tree to tree; the long body of a snake, gliding across a bare floor; a group of elephants, meeting in the forest, touching each other gently with their trunks, greeting, welcoming, making friends.

He had been in the wild places. He had seen the great ones of the earth, in their splendour and majesty. He couldn't talk about it.

'It was OK, Mum,' he said. 'Everything was OK.'

Elizabeth Laird
Wild Things 2:
BABOON ROCK

Deep in the African bush! It'll be the best birthday of Afra's life.

Her present is a trip to Baboon Rock, living in the wild among elephants, cheetahs and zebra. Tom and Joseph are sharing the adventure and, best of all, her busy father is coming too.

But her dad breaks his promise. And Afra's disappointment makes her disobey all the rules. After dark, she creeps out alone, desperate to save a baby baboon. And herself becomes the prey of some hungry night hunters . . .

Elizabeth Laird
**Wild Things 4:
RHINO FIRE**

It is the rhino's only chance of survival . . .

As the animal charges away from the speeding helicopter,
Titus leans perilously out to take aim with his long dart gun.
If only the rare black rhino can be relocated to a new reserve,
Afra and Joseph know it might join the few others of its kind.

But at Nakuru the rhino faces a far greater danger. Men
armed with powerful rifles, who will kill it for its valuable
horn. And who are ready to shoot any child that tries to
stop them . . .

WILD THINGS titles
available from Macmillan

The prices shown below are correct at the time of going to press. However, Macmillan Publishers reserve the right to show new retail prices on covers which may differ from those previously advertised.

ELIZABETH LAIRD

1. Leopard Trail	0 330 37148 7	£2.99
2. Baboon Rock	0 330 37149 5	£2.99
3. Elephant Thunder	0 330 37150 9	£2.99
4. Rhino Fire	0 330 37151 7	£2.99

All Macmillan titles can be ordered at your local bookshop or are available by post from:

Book Service by Post
PO Box 29, Douglas, Isle of Man IM99 1BQ

Credit cards accepted. For details:
Telephone: 01624 675137
Fax: 01624 670923
E-mail: bookshop@enterprise.net

Free postage and packing in the UK.
Overseas customers: add £1 per book (paperback)
and £3 per book (hardback).